Valentine's Day Dinner

Joe Garri

Illustrations by

Gabrielle Muñoz

Valentine's Day Dinner

A Short Story
A Long, Short Story
A Long, Short, Love Story

Joe Garri

This is a work of fiction. All the characters, organizations, and events portrayed in this novel are either products of the author's imagination or are used fictitiously. Any resemblance to actual events, locales, or persons, living or dead, is coincidental.

VALENTINE'S DAY DINNER
by Joe Garri
FIC027000 FICTION / Romance / General
FIC027020 FICTION / Romance / Contemporary
FIC000000 FICTION / General
ISBN: 979-8-88636-012-7 (paperback)
ISBN: 979-8-88636-013-4 (hardcover)
ISBN: 979-8-88636-014-1 (ebook)

Original cover illustrations by Gabrielle Muñoz

Cover design by Lewis Agrell

Authority Publishing
11230 Gold Express Drive, #310-413
Gold River, CA 95670

Printed in the United States of America

May God grant us the wisdom
to embrace all of his gifts,
including and especially
those sent in the wrong gift boxes.

Joe Garri
1/1/2023

Dedication

This story is dedicated to KL,
a most enchanting girl
who is genuinely deserving of
true love, everlasting bliss,
and living happily ever after.

Table of Contents

CHAPTER 1

Frank and Betty

Frank Mako stopped writing and looked out the window of his hotel room. It was the middle of the afternoon. A light snow was falling, and it looked bitter cold outside. A bit earlier, Frank had submitted a proposal for cognitive consideration via text message and was anxious to get the answer, as he could not finish the story he was writing without it. However, Betty Trulovke was taking her time and had not yet responded.

The arc of every great love story ever told, be it fictional or real, always features the two lovers eventually getting to the point where their feelings become so intense, one of the pair becomes afraid and runs away. Eventually, the scared lover realizes that the act of leaving forfeits the chance at true love and returns to consummate the relationship. The alternative ending is that the scared lover chooses *not* to return, either due to fear or some other reason, leading to the great tragedy of potential true love left unrealized. Frank and Betty's story had followed this arc to the letter, albeit at an accelerated rate, as they had partaken of this dance many times before. The only thing left to be decided in this particular iteration was the ending.

As he waited for the answer, Frank stood by the window and watched the snow fall while he pondered on the last several months. He was looking at an almost empty parking lot, which at the opposite end had a single-story building that he had seen before, but only in pictures. As he looked out the window, Frank thought about the strange turn of events that ended with him being there, in this life, at this time.

Frank considered himself a fallen or at least a demoted angel. His heart was pure, and he strived always to be honorable and do the right thing. However, he had learned by experience that to fulfill his true destiny and be ready for her, he would have to learn certain devilish wooing techniques and amorous tricks of the trade that pleased all women. Just in case she would also be pleased, he wanted to learn them so as to be ready. He had been an earnest pupil and had mastered his lessons but had endured an angelic demerit in the process. Thus, he now saw himself as an angel with a busted wing, sort of rough around the edges and a bit worn and scarred. He always hoped his demerit would not have been in vain and that someday he would find her and reap the desired rewards by making use of the techniques learned. However, as time passed, Frank was not so sure this would be the case, at least in this lifetime. Frank had always been of a very optimistic disposition, but now, after waiting for her all this time, he was beginning to lose hope.

In this life, Frank had been born a healer and a sculptor of sorts. With his hands, he was able to erase or improve imperfections of form, healing the bearers in turn and sculpting their souls in the process. Frank found great pleasure in his work. By the time he met Betty, Frank was very content with his vocation and accomplishments; yet he remained unfulfilled. In his heart he always knew the reason why. Despite a lifetime of tireless searching, sadly Frank had not yet found her. Frank's secret prayer of someday being able to find his true love, the one meant for him, had not yet been answered. She had not yet materialized.

In his deepest essence, Frank had a creative streak. That side of him was always at the core no matter the external wrappings he was born in. He had previously been born an actor, a dancer, a poet, and a musician. Frank had composed many a sonnet, poem, opera, and ballad in other lives. In this life, his most creative creation was a manuscript that he had been working on for twenty-five years and which he had just finished writing, but somehow could not finish editing.

Frank surmised that the problem was a lack of inspiration. He somehow could not quiet his mind long enough to get in touch with his creative side. The cares and concerns of daily living always seemed to get in the way. Thus, he found himself stuck, and not able to complete the task. Like a soldier without a country or a knight without a lady, Frank had no muse whose inspiration would prompt him to finish his book. Before Frank met Betty, he found himself in a rut—stuck, frustrated, and utterly unable to get himself out of it.

One day, as was his habit when he needed to clear his mind of mundane concerns, Frank found himself perusing through a multitude of sirens and their calls. One in particular caught his eye. He did not recognize her at first, but her beaming smile and the honest and innocent way she displayed her imperfections called to him deeply, viscerally. At first glance, she did not seem a suitable suitor, as she appeared way too young and seemed to have a multitude of children and dogs. Since the creation of time, Frank had only owned one dog and had always aspired to have one male child of his own. A son whom he could nurture and teach what he knew, the wisdom he had learned through many years of study and of searching for "her." He did not necessarily see himself undertaking the care of any other live pets nor the critter creations of other humans.

However, the more Frank heard her siren call, the more drawn to her he became. After telling himself that she was not the one for him, he took a calculated chance at a short, friendly exchange of innocent, flirtatious banter. After all, he needed and wanted to practice his flirting skills and be ready for if and when she came. What happened next was utterly unexpected. Their interaction formed a grip on his heart that has grown ever since and has a hold on him to this day.

It turns out that Betty was from God's country, where salt-of-the-earth type people hail from. Frank had always been drawn to God's country and God's people, as every iteration of her over his lifetimes had come from there. The more he learned, the more intrigued Frank became. Betty described herself as an "old soul," but Frank soon realized she was best described as a woman with the soul of a child. She was beautiful but did not seem to know it. She was innocent, trusting, and had a strong desire to please others. Betty very much loved her family and was very fond of all children. Moreover, she had the integrity to stand by what is right despite incurring the risk of negative personal consequences. When Frank learned that Betty did not have children of her own and only had one dog named Mildred, he worried that he might inadvertently have ventured into unsafe ground and might someday find himself in deep trouble. Alas, by then it was too late. Frank found himself powerless to do anything else but to continue the course. By then he was committed. By then he was trapped.

The first time he spoke to her on the phone, Frank thought he had a sudden realization of who she might be. Her voice was like that of an angel he once knew—an angel he had always known. It was as if the vibrations of her voice were at such a pitch and contained certain tones that only his dog ears could hear them. The way she said normal, everyday phrases like "Hi," and "Good day," was as if Frank had never heard them uttered since the beginning of creation. At the end of the conversation, Frank was left as drawn to her as he was left confused, wondering if this could really be her, his one true love for whom he had waited his entire life. He pondered possibilities as he drifted off to sleep, running the conversation time and time again in his head.

During that first phone call, Betty was as engaging and endearing as she was intriguing. With great ease and honesty, she exposed herself, not in form but in a deeper sense, explaining her previous challenges, her current fears, and her longings to find herself and where she truly belonged, both geographically and with whom. Betty explained to Frank how she had recently moved out of the city by the great lake and was temporarily staying back at her hometown at her parents' house until she figured out her next move. She shared that she was a snowbird in training and was considering the land that protrudes into the sea as a living destination, particularly if she found someone there who would convince her to stay. Betty was in the process of planning a trip south for the winter so that she and Mildred could experience what it was like to live in a warmer clime. During their conversation she, in passing, revealed her disappointment and dismay with a prior love affair at not being prioritized during a most important event for her: Valentine's Day dinner.

Frank listened intently and upon ending the conversation, pondered her words. Frank was engulfed by a deep sense of optimism at the thought that he might meet her someday. He longed to meet her, to hold her, to kiss her. Frank suddenly got a strange feeling, almost as if he had been sent on a very special mission. Right then and there, he decided to do anything in his power to convince her to stay, if for no other reason than to show her that there would be someone who would want her to. Right then and there, he made the commitment to do everything in his power to grant her explicit request, to answer her secret prayer. It felt almost as if an irresistible power unbeknown to him directed him to do so. These thoughts and yearnings were somewhat alarming to Frank, as making rash decisions of any kind was not in his nature. Frank consciously convinced himself that these thoughts were mere meaningless musings. He then made the commitment that in future dealings with Betty, he would restrain his heart's irresistible urge to leap.

As the bonding and sharing continued, Frank could not help but become more and more engrossed in her, in the essence of her. The more Frank learned about Betty, the more he wanted to know. His mind began to see the limitless possibilities of past and future lives, of multitudes of universes that exist parallel to this one. Frank felt that he wanted to share as well; he wanted her to know who he was. He sent her a couple of chapters from his manuscript that spoke of him and of his nature. As this connection that Frank and Betty made grew and cemented, Frank's horizons expanded; he dared think of potential possibilities. His heart rejoiced at what could be. When Betty shared with Frank that she and Mildred were planning a trip to the land that protrudes into the sea for the winter, Frank became overjoyed and eagerly invited her to consider a short detour to his tropical city by the sea so they could meet.

Eventually the pictures came, slowly at first and then at a faster clip. They were as engaging and anticipated as they were confusing. In some, Betty was smiling and radiating such energy that Frank was sure it was her, the one he had always known. There were others in which she was not smiling that showed a harder, sharper edge to her that Frank did not recognize. Then he remembered the stories she had told him about her illness, her suffering as a young woman, and the scars that she faced in the mirror every day as a reminder of her past. Frank understood and came to the realization that each and every side of her was part of the whole, and that he would be happy to have her no matter any physical or mental peculiarities. If she were her, he would gladly and adoringly kiss each and every one of the scars on her face and body, as they in part made her who she was in this life.

Slowly at first, but eventually with the certainty of a chill that creeps into the body heralding an impending fever, Frank realized that he himself had changed. He began listening to music more intently, his step was brisker, colors seemed brighter, he saw the actions of others in a kinder light. He began to speak in songs and experienced a side of himself that was utterly unfamiliar. Frank began to feel with confidence that the universe was conspiring to ensure his happiness, their happiness. He felt creative again. He was able to quiet his mind. He was able to write. His language became flowery and the structure of it changed. In essence, Frank felt he was living inspired. He liked himself best when he lived inspired. As Frank in this life was a writer at heart, he lived in his head. When Frank lived inspired, he was able to conjure up a uniquely exquisite blend of the past, present, and future in a beautiful collage of crisp, bright, and harmonious colors. Living inspired humanized him, this demoted angel with a busted wing.

Frank gladly and eagerly took risks and chances at the possibility of what could be. During a trip to the land of the cowboys to accompany her Granny, Betty mentioned that she had not read his chapters because she had to do it on her phone, the task made difficult due to the small print. Upon hearing Betty say this, Frank promptly commissioned a magic tablet built specifically for her, in a color that he knew she would love. He had her name engraved on it. When she mentioned how important Valentine's Day dinner was to her, Frank immediately made plans to whisk her away for that event to one of his favorite places, the last island at the end of the road in the middle of the sea. He made dinner reservations at his favorite restaurant there. After all, Valentine's Day was fast approaching—only a mere few months away. Frank did all these things without ever having met Betty, but he did it gladly to be ready just in case, for losing this grand opportunity was utterly unthinkable.

Then they met. When she stepped out of her carriage, Frank recognized her immediately. Betty did not seem to recognize him for who he really was, but their dog did. Mildred instantly recognized his scent; the wagging of her tail showed how glad she was to see an old lost friend once again. Frank tried to be as unthreatening and friendly as possible, but Betty did not seem afraid or concerned in any way. Upon meeting Betty, Frank tried to kiss her on the cheek, but at the last second, she shifted her head and kissed him on the lips. The kiss sent an electric shock through him, resulting in a momentary loss of balance, necessitating Frank to brace himself against Betty with a hug.

Frank had carefully planned everything for Betty's visit, lest she be scared off and run away. He had cleared space for her at his castle in the clouds and had intentions of a slow reintroduction for the two of them, which included her sleeping in the bedroom while he slept on the couch. He brought written proof that he was harmless and placed it inside an envelope on her nightstand, with instructions to open the envelope only if she began to develop feelings for him. Despite his best intentions to keep his distance and maintain a certain level of gentlemanly etiquette, Frank found himself pulled by an insurmountable force, which made it extremely difficult for him to leave her side. However, he persisted and finally was able to tear himself away and keep his promise to her of acting gentlemanly and exhibiting proper etiquette. He wanted her to know that he always kept his promises. Frank had always strived to be honorable and do the right thing. In this instance and despite his best efforts, he almost failed.

The next four days were as heavenly as the two following were sad. Their first meal was, as per her request, food from the sea, and it took place on his balcony. While dining, Frank learned more about Betty and felt himself falling deeper and deeper into a bottomless abyss. They eventually migrated to the bedroom, where Frank planned a kiss good night and a quick escape. Frank found it extremely hard to leave her side but did so, comforted by the thought that he would get to see her again the following morning. He was not so naïve as to think that Betty had not experienced life fully, but secretly hoped that there was a part of her yet untouched. Perhaps a side of her she was not aware of and which only he could bring to life. After all, he had studied and learned devilish amorous techniques so as to give her that exquisite experience once he found her. He had learned all that and much more for her. That night Frank realized that he would be willing to do anything for Betty, except to hurt her. Hurting her had never been part of the plan or his intentions, as Frank had been born with a heart devoid of cruelty.

For her part, Mildred took to Frank as a lost dog takes to her true master. Betty confided in Frank that she always expected to own a larger, better-behaved dog, but had fallen in love with Mildred after getting to know her. Betty had eventually decided to adopt Mildred and become a dog mom. Betty told Frank that Mildred had changed her life in many wonderful ways. Frank knew why this was the case, for Mildred was his dog—their dog. He had owned her at one point, ages ago, and had come across her multiple times in many different lives but had not for a while now. In this life, Frank had settled for carefree, magical pets—colorful, digital fish that danced for him nights when he was alone. They were ever-present when he was at home and made occasional appearances in his dreams, as if to remind him of his lost dog.

In this life, Mildred had been born a domesticated animal, but she was a hunting dog at heart. Eons ago, Frank had found her as a pup, lost in the wilderness after being separated from her mother. Frank took her in, cared for her, made her his own. Nowadays, Mildred was much better behaved but at times the frustrations of having lost her true master got the best of her, particularly when she was around the small, loud-mouthed ankle-biters who occasionally got on her nerves. If she ran into them while feeling gloomy, Mildred's first instinct was to eat them, particularly if they were really small and looked like rabbits. During one of their conversations, Betty shared with Frank the story about a scary incident months prior which involved Mildred becoming aggressive toward a tiny dog, which very much looked like a rabbit. Upon hearing this story and Betty's occasional unease when she brought Mildred around small dogs, Frank smiled knowingly. He was well aware of the tricks that God played sometimes. He knew from personal experience how at times God granted our most ardent wishes but sent them in the wrong gift boxes.

The next three days and nights included plenty of quality time together after work, and quiet dinners, each becoming more enjoyable in turn as Frank learned more and more about Betty. While dining with her, Frank was enthralled by the light that shone inside Betty, obscuring all her battle scars from view, and allowing her to show herself to him as the glorious being that she was. Frank was mesmerized listening to Betty, happy that he had finally found her. Looking at Betty, Frank was reminded of the love name he had always called her: "Baby girl." Love is eternal but the spoken language is not. Long before any language was ever spoken and prior to the Tower of Babel crashing down, he always called her a variation of that name. Frank always saw her as a stunningly spectacular specimen of female beauty, harboring the heart and soul of a child. Her physical form called to him, her mind fascinated him, her demeanor enthralled him…her innocence redeemed him.

On the morning of the fourth day when Betty wanted to explore a longer walk to the ocean with their dog, Frank was worried and felt compelled to follow in his carriage to make sure she made it to her destination safely. Like a guardian angel, he hovered and made sure no harm came to her. Frank was worried about doing this, as Betty had mentioned a prior incident where a previous lover had shown up to her morning walk unannounced, the act causing her considerable trepidation. Frank hoped she would not take his actions in the same light. If discovered, he hoped she would forgive him, as he meant her no harm. Hurting her was never part of the plan nor the intentions that Frank had toward Betty, as Frank in this life had been born with a heart devoid of cruelty.

When Frank finally saw Betty reach the boardwalk by the sea and knew she was safe, he intended to turn around and go, but somehow felt the need to let her know he had been there. She heard his call, answered it, and came to him. The sight of her—a tall, beautiful, blonde girl glistening in the sun—made his heart sing at the realization that he had finally found her in this life, as he always hoped he would. Still, Betty did not seem to recognize him as her own true love. Mildred did and eagerly wagged her tail, so as to make the point.

That entire day Frank's mood could best be described as sublime. He texted with Betty several times and informed her that he would be having dinner with his sister, as he did every Tuesday. He invited Betty to join. Frank had always been very secretive about his affairs, and never brought lovers around his family except on a handful of occasions—and then only after having known them for a long time. That day he felt no hesitation. After all, he had known Betty for all of eternity and in many different previous lives. He wanted to see if his sister would recognize her too. He was sure she would, just as he was sure his niece Kassy would find in Betty a kindred spirit, and they would become the best of friends, like they had always been.

Frank's sister, Chloe, not having yet met Betty, warned Frank to be careful, as they had just recently met. Chloe knew her brother to be a hopeless romantic who had been waiting a lifetime to find his true love. She warned him to make sure before he let his heart take flight. Most importantly, Chloe did not want her brother to be hurt like she knew he could be. Chloe also worried about Betty, as she knew that Betty and her brother were just beginning to get to know one another. Chloe advised Frank to go slow, as it was not fair for him to put Betty in a difficult position and have her face undue duress, unless he was sure it was her. Upon his insistence, Chloe promised Frank she would keep an open mind and told him she looked forward to meeting Betty. She asked Frank to invite Betty to a family gathering taking place that weekend so that Betty could meet her, Kassy, and Kassy's two critters: Little Myla and Baby Jax.

The whole time Frank was eating with his sister, he kept looking at the doorway of the restaurant, expecting Betty to walk through at any moment, as he had invited her to come and hoped she would. His heart leaped with joy every time the door opened but alas, she never came. Toward the end of the meal, Frank glanced at his phone only to realize he had missed several texts from Betty in which she at first asked if she could still come to dinner, but then eventually texted that she would stay home. Frank was immediately saddened by the texts as he remembered how, in many previous interactions with Betty in many prior lives, desired wishes and intentions had been unnecessarily thwarted by poor timing, missed opportunities, and wrong interpretations. Frank promised himself that he would not allow that to ever happen again. He ordered a meal for Betty so that he could bring it home to her. Frank indeed saw himself as a demoted angel, but also as a protector and a provider. Bringing Betty a meal which he had procured by the fruit of his labor made him happy; it made him feel whole, needed—useful.

That evening, upon entering his castle, Frank found Mildred, as usual, standing by the doorway. She leaped at him with joy the moment he entered the threshold. Initially, Frank did not see Betty in the room and his heart sank at not seeing her there. It felt like he had just experienced another strange premonition about Betty. He then realized that although the occasion might one day come where Betty would leave him, she would never leave without Mildred. She would never leave their dog behind. Betty was indeed there, all along, lying on the couch. She had been reading his two chapters, which he had printed for her that morning and placed alongside the sealed envelope on her nightstand. Frank had hoped that reading the two chapters would spark the flame of recognition in her and that Betty would remember him for who he was—remember them for who they were. They did not, and she did not, although he came to know eventually that she had been deeply moved by what she had learned from reading them.

That night, Frank watched Betty eat the meal he had brought her while they both drank wine. They talked about deeper subjects, about themselves. Frank felt that this exchange of ideas as to proper etiquette and behavior toward one another brought them emotionally much closer to each other. That night, they deeply bonded. Talking and listening to Betty intently, for the first time during her visit, Frank felt as if Betty and he made a deep psychological connection and were now emotionally becoming one. This was the moment that Frank had hoped for since he felt their initial connection, that first time he spoke to her on the phone and first heard her voice. Perhaps even from the first time he had ever laid eyes on her, many lifetimes ago.

In this life, Betty had been born chatty. During the previous four nights, while dining and engaging in conversation, she spoke incessantly, seemingly without end. She would occasionally ask Frank for his thoughts on certain topics, only to mostly ignore him when he tried to offer his opinion and continue her chatting and pontificating. As for Frank, he was happy to just sit there, mesmerized, and listen. Having been born an introvert, Frank lived in an extroverted world and by the time he got home in the evening, he had already exhausted the meager allotment of words he felt compelled to utter each day. At night, he was most happy to have someone to listen to, be captivated by, and engrossed in. Like he had always done every time he had been lucky enough to find her, he would sit by her and listen to her every utterance with deep interest, as he felt an insatiable desire to know everything about her.

However, after that fourth night, Frank felt compelled to speak, to share. To tell her what he knew of himself, of her, and of them both. Betty kept her secrets in a pouch, which she kept in her nightstand drawer. Frank kept his secrets in his heart, but he was once again ready to share them with her, especially now that he was sure he had found her. Frank longed to tell Betty that he had learned much in this life that could be of use to her. In his sleep that night and during the entire following day, Frank could think of nothing but the many things he wanted to share with Betty.

After years of diligent scientific pursuits, Frank learned that certain conditions are physiological, yet affected profoundly by someone's state of mind. Frank longed to tell Betty that he had learned that certain burdens, including the one she carried, affected primarily women and it was thought that it had to do with their hormonal constitution. Besides the current dogma that certain physical conditions affect the mind, Frank was convinced that the reverse was also true. He subscribed to the theory that if the mind was healed and healthy, physical conditions would ameliorate and be easier to bear. He was of the opinion that women had to be tended to, cared for—watered, in a sense. If they were not they, like plants, would wither away and fail to thrive—not physically, but spiritually. Frank longed to share with Betty his theory that perhaps her burden and its consequences would improve in a better clime and if she were tended to properly. His plans were to do just that, to tend to her and her needs so that she would never feel alone, never feel disowned.

Frank wanted to tell Betty that perhaps the reason why she got sick every October was not, as she thought, because that month heralded the beginning of winter. Perhaps it was because October was her birth month. Perhaps she was getting sick due to the emotional turmoil over the fact that another year had come and gone without her finding her true love, the one meant exclusively for her. Frank was familiar with this angst from personal experience, as he had endured the same type of feelings year after year himself around the day of his birth, in this life and in many others, while patiently waiting for her to appear and reveal herself to him.

Frank longed to tell Betty that due to his prior academic pursuits, he had befriended two wizards who could be of assistance with some of her other concerns. One was in the tropical city by the sea and could fill in the small, infertile areas of her scalp that although miniscule in size, Betty had shared with Frank were the cause of considerable emotional consternation. The other lived in the city where the stars lived upon the hills and had devoted his entire life to the study of that which encased the form. Perhaps he could help with her scars. If there was ever someone who might have the knowledge and skills to be able to help, Frank knew it would be this wizard, as his magic and potions were most powerful. Frank knew both of these wizards and could arrange for Betty to be seen by them at any time.

Most importantly, Frank longed to tell her that even he, himself, could help. After many years of study and practice, he had developed the knowledge and skills to grant her a great gift. With the help of a magic wand, which he had procured at considerable expense, his skills, and his hands, Frank was in a position to grant Betty that which by now he had learned was one of her biggest wishes. He could grant her a body that any dress or any man would love to hug. She would be set free of the worry of having to shop and dress for her body type. She could wear any dress, matched with the appropriate pair of shoes, and look like he always saw her, spectacularly beautiful… stunning.

Frank would share with Betty that although he was not a rich man, he had saved enough for her to have most of what she seemed to want. He could afford to give her a larger castle in an even higher cloud, from where she would have a better view of the bay and of the large, floating cities that danced by daily on their way out to sea, for which she seemed to have developed a strange fascination. A park was being built across the street from where he lived. There, Mildred could run free, undisturbed by the small ankle-biter tormentors, some of which looked like rabbits. Frank could afford to grant Betty the carriage of her dreams, which she had pointed out to him one day while strolling together. He could grant her all that and much more. He could teach her much and in turn, learn much from her. They could learn together, live together, love together for all time as they always had before, as was their destiny now that he had found her.

The fifth day following their fourth night together, with all these thoughts swirling around in his head, Frank walked on air. Surely, Betty had felt the connection too. Deep in her mind she must have recognized at least a part of him. A memory of him had surely been awakened in the deep recesses of her heart. He had seen it on her face; he was sure of it. He had recognized the look in her eyes. The fifth day after the fourth night, Frank was sure in his step, steady in his resolve, and totally convinced that now he had found her, all would be fine. Until it wasn't.

Upon arriving from work on the fifth night, all seemed as usual at first until Betty informed Frank that she wanted to talk to him, but it could wait until after dinner. His heart skipped upon hearing her words as simultaneously, a memory rose deep inside him. He remembered having this conversation with her before—many, many times before—in many different lives and throughout time. He knew what was to come just as he also knew that he would be helpless to stop or change it. Frank had tried to convince her to stay countless times before and most times he had failed. Resolving himself to his fate, he showered, got dressed for dinner, and took her to the next restaurant he wanted Betty to experience. It was an outdoor café adjacent to a marina located within walking distance from where he lived.

Dinner on that fifth night was as always. Betty talked and Frank listened. He tried to be as she would have expected him to be and acted as before. However, he did not dare utter a word of everything he had dreamt that day that he would tell her, of all the things he wanted to share, of all the secrets he wanted to divulge. While he listened to her, Frank's mind went back to that morning. Before leaving for work, he inadvertently had knocked off the dining room table a small notebook that belonged to Betty. As he bent over to pick it up from the floor, his eyes looked upon two phrases she had written on the top of the page that had randomly landed facing him.

Frank felt guilty at reading something that Betty had not voluntarily shared, but now desperately looking for a lifeboat, he thought perhaps this was a message God had sent him. After all, the notebook had landed randomly with that page on top in such a way so as to allow him to see what was written on it. Frank was well aware that God occasionally would send messages in the most peculiar of ways to those he was trying to influence or help. Out of the blue and as if in passing, he blurted out the second phrase at her, hoping that she would somehow understand God's message and respond accordingly. Betty looked at him slightly perplexed but did not respond at all. Frank desisted and did not try further. Eventually, he came to learn that those two phrases referred to books that Betty had been advised to read.

Frank braced himself for what was to come and hoped for the best. On the way back from the restaurant, he walked back with her, desperately hoping that it would not be the last time she walked beside him in this life. They engaged in casual conversation as if nothing was amiss, and Frank hoped against all hope that she wanted to talk to him about something else, other than what he knew was to come.

That day, Betty wore particularly high heels and stood almost as tall as he, perhaps even taller. As she walked tall and proud, Betty said that high heels made her feel powerful, as they allowed her to deal with men eye to eye. Betty told Frank that high heels gave her the feeling that she had girl ogle power—she pronounced it "girl oogle power." Betty shared with Frank that in high heels, she felt invincible.

When the excuses came out of her mouth as to why she had to leave, he knew them to be such. Frank told Betty that she did not have to have a reason, for he understood everything and already knew what the reason was. She had unwillingly divulged it to him on the way to the restaurant; but that did not matter, as he had always known. He knew even before he had seen her again, as the reason was always the same. However, in this life Betty had been born with a pleasing disposition and she did not want to hurt him, so excuses she made up as best she could. Betty spoke of how much she had enjoyed the few days they had spent together, and freely expressed her gratitude to Frank for having treated her and Mildred so well during their visit. Frank in turn, consciously deluded himself into partially believing that her excuses were the real reasons she had chosen to leave. He hoped against all hope that there was something he could do to stop her, to get her to change her mind. After all, after that first night on the phone with her, he had already committed himself to doing everything in his power to try to convince her to stay. Frank once again experienced the strange feeling as if he had been sent on a mission to grant her explicit request, to answer her secret prayer.

Frank did not sleep that night. He reviewed in his head all the events that took place the previous twenty-four hours in search for the reason for Betty's abrupt change of plans. Deep in his heart, he already knew the reason, but at the same time felt some ambivalence. He was afraid to ask her specifically as he knew she would not tell him the truth. At that time, she would or could not face it. During the night, he struggled to think of anything else he could do to make her change her mind. Frank ventured an offer to cover the expenses for another accommodation in the tropical city by the sea so that she could remain close to him for a couple of weeks longer. That way they could continue the love pirouette that they were currently engaged in, thus buying him a little more time so that he could show himself to her as he really was. He wrote her a note explaining his offer and left it on her nightstand the following morning. He placed it in an envelope along with the funds required to cover the costs involved. Frank knew that Betty would refuse his offer, but he felt there was no other move left for him to try.

The morning of the sixth day, Frank left for his daily toil sad, and was sad all day. Before leaving for work, Frank and Betty ate breakfast together in the dining room. While doing so, Betty had looked out the balcony glass door and commented as to how gloomy and foggy it looked outside. Frank thought that the weather that morning mirrored exactly how he felt in his heart. During the day, Frank texted with Betty several times and expressed his desire for her happiness and told her that he understood her decision. He told her that he was ready to move mountains so that they could be together but the one thing he could not and would not fight was her will. If she wished to go, he was powerless to stop her. He had always respected her decisions and was very much aware how much Betty detested those who did not take her seriously or were quick to discard her opinion. Frank would never make that mistake, not because of the way she felt, but rather because of the way *he* felt. Frank had always looked at Betty as his partner and equal, walked side by side with her, and had known her to be intelligent and of good judgment. It was obvious that Betty was struggling with her decision to leave; Frank knew that he owed her the decency of allowing her the emotional space to make up her mind without any meddling from him.

When Betty vacillated, as Frank knew she would, and told him she was torn, he responded by telling her that if she had already made up her mind to leave and felt strongly about it, then she should go. He knew that if he somehow convinced her to stay now at the last minute, she would eventually end up resenting him for doing so, and their friendship would end. After many interactions with Betty throughout time, Frank knew that the only chance he had at having her return to him was to let her go now, no matter the pain it might cause him.

That sixth night when he got home, her things were packed. Frank was as sad to see this, as he was glad she was still there so that he could hold her one last time before she left. They once again walked Mildred together. Afterward, he helped her get the things down to her carriage. Before she left, he could not help but tell her how sad he was that she was leaving and how much she inspired him. Betty kissed Frank on the lips like the first time they met, hugged him, and got into the driver's seat. He walked downstairs to open the garage door gate for her so that she could leave.

Frank stood by the gate as Betty drove by; she gave him a half-smile, and left. Her face at that time seemed stern and resolved, like the unsmiling pictures she had sent him weeks prior. The only sadness Frank saw was in Mildred's eyes. Their dog seemed to sense something was amiss and looked sorry to leave him. Betty made leaving Frank that day look effortless and easy. He wished she would have tried to make it seem a little harder.

Frank walked upstairs to replace the dolly he had used to carry her things. As he did so, and to comfort himself in the thought that he had done everything possible to convince her to stay, Frank replayed all his prior moves in his mind. He had not been as smart as Odysseus in figuring out a way to prevent falling prey to her siren call, but then missing the opportunity to see her once again was unthinkable, no matter how much pain her leaving was sure to cause him. He then mused as to how once again he had been cast as Cyrano. Frank was happy to play that role, for at least with Cyrano, his beloved had eventually recognized who he was, albeit in the final moments before Cyrano's death. Frank resigned himself to his fate and the fact that once again, as he had done time and time again in many lifetimes, he had found and potentially lost her. God had played a trick on them all right.

Frank did not sleep that night. He tossed and turned, waiting for her to text him and tell him she had reached her destination safely, as this had become her usual norm when traveling. This night she did not do that. As per Betty's request before she left, Frank had promised her that he would not reach out, and that he would give her whatever time and space she told him she needed. He hoped that she would somehow miss him enough to give him another try. He desperately wished it so.

The morning of the seventh day, Frank arose later than usual, now living uninspired. He was tired but somehow, he could not rest. He could not quiet his mind and knew that day he could not write, even if he wanted to. Frank had still not heard from Betty and wondered if she had made it to her destination safely, after driving several hours that night. His services as a guardian angel were no longer desired, but he was a guardian angel still, the one with the busted wing. As he thought about it, Frank saw no harm in reaching out one last time to make sure she was safe and well. He reached out that morning, to which she responded with one curt text saying that she was okay. Frank resigned himself to not hearing again from Betty, at least for a while. He comforted himself with the thought that perhaps she would eventually feel the need to contact him again.

The afternoon of the seventh day, Frank found himself in the place where he routinely performed his magic when Betty texted him saying that she hoped that he was having a good day and that she missed him. His heart leaped out of his chest at reading her message, and he lived inspired for the rest of the day. Similar communications followed on the next day and the following day after that. Frank's hopes rose with each and every text, only to be dimmed by remembering that this was a normal routine of separations. When the emotional fire had been felt intensely enough, it was always hard to separate completely in an abrupt manner. There were always yearnings to see, touch, feel the person whom one had separated from. Frank knew it, as he had experienced this with her before. Although still living inspired at times when she texted, he resigned himself to adjusting his thoughts, curing his mind. In summary, Frank finally decided it was time to mentally move on. This decision was difficult because Betty's texts continued to trickle in occasionally as the weeks went on.

Every time Betty texted Frank that she missed him, he wanted to respond that he missed her twice as much. That of all of the world's problems, missing him was the easiest to fix. He wanted to tell her that anytime she wanted to reach out, she could just text him. Anytime she wanted to talk, all she had to do was call him. If the time ever came that she wanted to see him, all she had to do was tell him and he would fix it. He would either go to where she was or have her brought to him by air, land, or sea. Her choice. Despite all he wanted to say, Frank thought it best to respond only by saying that he missed her too.

In this life, Frank had been born his father's son. Like his father, Frank aspired to be honorable, dependable, and always do the right thing. He desired to be a good friend to all. While searching for ways to cure his mind, Frank thought that perhaps in this life, he had been born to be Betty's friend. Just like Charles, a high school friend on whom she knew she could always count. Or perhaps like her friend Cheryl, on whom she could confide all her secrets, and who, like her guardian angel, always knew her location, lest harm come to her. It then occurred to Frank that perhaps that was his mission in this life, to be Betty's friend.

He thought perhaps someday he could be like a Charles to Betty. Yes, maybe someday he could make that right, except that "right" could not be right now. Right now, his feelings for Betty were too intense, too reptilian, too primal. Right now, the conversation he wanted to have with Betty was much deeper, piercing—a conversation of a different nature altogether. But perhaps someday, whether weeks, months, years, or as he feared, centuries or millennia from now, his feelings would eventually fade enough so that Frank could be a Charles or a Cheryl to Betty. Now he could not, as his feelings for Betty were too powerful and passionate to be just her friend.

In this life, Frank had been born to be responsible and safe. Texting while driving was not his norm, but as weeks passed, he could not keep his gaze off his phone anytime he received a text, hoping it was her. One morning several weeks later, while Frank was driving to work, his phone showed a text which at initial glance alarmed him. While driving, he somehow read that Betty had sustained cramps that had caused her to lose consciousness, and she had ended up at the hospital where she had been told that things did not look good. At reading this, his initial instinct was to steer his steed in her direction. To mount his horse, his carriage, or a magic carpet, and ride to her. He would tend to her, care for her, make her well. If God's plan was to take Betty, he would rip her from his arms if that was what it took. He immediately called her.

Frank felt silly when Betty told him that he had misread the text. She had texted that Gramps had lost consciousness, had sustained some trauma in the fall, and at the hospital her family was warned that the situation did not look good, as his health was already frail. Betty was waiting to hear from her family as to Gramps' progress and was readying to return home if his condition worsened. Frank had never met Betty's grandfather, but his heart went out to him, nonetheless. Gramps was from God's country and was one of the salt-of-the-earth type people who hailed from there. Frank liked him just because of that and because he was one of her kinfolk. Frank had always liked all of her kinfolk if for no other reason than they were all somewhat responsible for her being born and becoming who she was. Frank wished nothing but the best for Gramps, and hoped he would have a full recovery. While speaking to Betty that morning, Frank once again felt the immense pull that her angelic voice had on him. He could not help but tell her so, but soon disengaged when he sensed that she wanted to.

By the time this phone call took place, Frank had resigned himself to the realization that he was not going to spend the upcoming Valentine's Day with Betty as he had hoped. However, Frank had not yet cancelled the reservations he had made on the small hope that somehow Betty would change her mind. That sense of optimism was renewed when Betty reached out to him via text regarding the news about Gramps. It then occurred to Frank that even if Betty changed her mind regarding his Valentine's Day plans, she might not be able to partake if Gramps' condition deteriorated and it became necessary for Betty to return home. He knew that having to return home prematurely, no matter the reason, would make Betty sad, as it would take away the joy she was currently experiencing at staying down south for the winter.

As these thoughts swirled around in his head, Frank got this strange premonition that Betty might reach out to him again in the future, like she had just done regarding the bad news about Gramps. Missing the opportunity to help or be with her, if indeed it presented itself, was unthinkable. While entertaining future possibilities of what might happen, thoughts poured into his mind all at once, as a river rushes downstream upon the rupture of a dam. Marinating on those thoughts, Frank's mind began to formulate preliminary potential plans for possible different future eventualities. That day Frank lived inspired—as if he had found the answer to every question, the key to every locked door.

As Frank pondered on potential future plans, it occurred to him that despite the many conversations he and Betty had shared during the first four days they spent together, there were still a lot of things he did not know about her. Some of that information would be of vital importance if Frank was to be in a position to help her, in the slim chance that she reached out after having to return back home. There had been times in prior lives when Frank needed information in order to be of service to Betty. It was usually times when Betty was in need of him, but somehow could not bring herself to ask for his help. In previous lives, he had resorted to buying the information, sending spies, traveling far and wide to find it, and even consulting shamans and wizards like Merlin. Frank marveled as to how easy it was to get that information in this life and at this time, as all the knowledge known to man—including Merlin's best kept secrets—could now be found on a magic tablet, which was at the reach of every man, woman, or child. As a matter of fact, Frank had commissioned a special one fashioned for Betty and expected it brought to him soon.

It took literally minutes in this life to find out all the information Frank needed about Betty. From pictures she had sent him, clues she had given him, and the use of the magic tablet, Frank found out much about Betty that he did not yet know. He learned that her parents were Miles and Lisa, that Betty's parents lived on Chase Street in a town in God's country, and that her middle name was Angela. The magic tablet allowed him to hover over her parents' house and clearly see the swing set in the back yard, as well as the gargantuan shed where her dad kept his car projects. He could see the field behind her house where Betty would have her walks with Mildred in the morning snow. He wondered if any dangers could lurk in wait for Betty there, but Frank knew that Mildred would always protect her, even when he could not, as it seemed his services as a guardian angel were no longer desired.

By comparing a picture Betty had sent him to hundreds of pictures of restaurants in the area, Frank was able to identify the restaurant named after another city, in a town named after someone, where Betty regularly ate with her relatives after church and important family functions. Betty had once told Frank about this restaurant as she was rushing to get ready for one of those dinners. She did not mention the restaurant by name but did mention that the town where the restaurant was located was halfway between here and there, by which she meant it was halfway from her parents' house—where she was staying—to the house of one of her two sisters, Jessica.

Later on that evening, Betty texted Frank a post-dinner picture of the gathering. The picture showed the happy family standing next to the table alongside one of the walls of the restaurant. The wall had very peculiar decorations and included a large window which reflected the white-brick decorations that stood opposite toward the entrance. It was this image that Frank compared to pictures of restaurants in the area that allowed him to figure out the name and location of the eatery in question. Frank knew that Betty would find peace and security in that establishment, as it had been the site of many enjoyable family gatherings throughout the years. If he were ever to suggest she go there, she would not be alarmed.

Like the time he inadvertently glanced at her notebook, Frank felt guilty about acquiring all this information about Betty without her first divulging it. Yet he reminded himself he was doing it for an honorable, chivalrous purpose. He wanted to be ready in case she called to him. He wanted to be able to go to her if she reached out to him. Frank liked living inspired because it allowed him to see all possibilities. As Valentine's Day approached, he saw many potential permutations of what might happen, and he wanted to be ready for all eventualities. If the opportunity arose for him to be of service to her, to be with her on that special night, missing that opportunity was unthinkable.

Several days later, while at a family gathering with Kassy's in-laws, Frank got a call from Betty. Frank's heart sprang when he saw the number on his phone. When he did not answer, she texted that she was checking in, as she had not done so in a while. Kassy and his sister Chloe both noticed his reaction, and both gave him a knowing smile. Frank did not want to be rude and answer a call in the middle of dinner so he texted Betty that dinner was almost over but that he would call her the minute he left the restaurant and started walking home. It was the same restaurant where Frank and Betty had eaten food from the sea together one of the first four days when she had visited. She replied in the affirmative and he immediately became impatient for the meal to be over so that he could talk to her. Still while sitting at the table, Frank texted Betty that he missed her and wished that she would have been there with him. Betty replied that she wished she were there too, and that she was sorry she had failed him. He responded by texting her not to worry, as Frank and Betty were, had always been, and would always be good.

Frank called Betty the moment he stepped out of the restaurant and was sorry to find that she did not answer and that her mailbox had not yet been set up, as she had recently purchased a new cell phone. He texted her to let her know that he was free for her to call, but she did not call. Frank figured that Betty had already fallen asleep and imagined that he would soon hear from her, but he did not. Without any explanation or apparent reason, Betty did not reach out for the next several weeks.

After several unanswered phone calls to Betty, Frank became increasingly worried. With every passing day, Frank became more and more concerned about not hearing from Betty, especially after the way their last interaction had ended where she seemed to express a desire to be with him. Frank fretted that something untoward had happened to her or maybe Gramps. He fought back every impulse he had to reach out to her further. He had promised her he would not do that, and it was important for Frank to let Betty know that he was a man of his word and that he kept his promises. He was afraid that if he were unable to keep his promise, Betty would think Frank untrustworthy and doubt him in the future. Her thinking that of him could potentially lead to the end of their friendship. Frank did not want that to happen.

However, Frank was now living inspired and was not without options as to how he could remedy the situation of not knowing about Betty. Living inspired allowed Frank to have an unlimited supply of ideas when it came to her. It seemed as if the well where those ideas originated was bottomless. It felt as if Frank had tapped into a much deeper stream of the eternal consciousness of everyone who has and will ever live, of everyone who has and will ever love. Living inspired, Frank felt as if he had found the answer to every question, the key to every locked door.

Frank decided to send carrier pigeons bearing gifts to find her. How Betty reacted to the gifts he sent would tell him a lot about her frame of mind and how she was feeling toward him. At first this attempt bore no fruit due to poor pigeon preparation and execution, but eventually, the pigeons got it right and she did respond positively to the gifts he sent. Frank was finally able to find out what had happened to Betty.

It turned out that Gramps had done well, but that other family matters needed attention unexpectedly. Betty felt compelled to be with her family and returned to the cold north. She returned to God's country, where she hailed from, but a place that now seemed eerily foreign to her. God's country now, especially in the cold, made her body ache, her mood swing in the wrong direction, and made her not feel herself. On her drive back to her family's home, she had regressed in her mind. She did not feel right and did not feel like she wanted to share this side of herself. Thus, she had not reached out to anyone, including Frank.

Upon confirming that Betty had returned home, Frank put into action the plan that he had tentatively formulated several weeks earlier when she texted the news about Gramps' fall and it became apparent that there was a possibility that she might have to return home. Frank sensed that Betty was not feeling herself now that she was back north. Moreover, Frank anticipated that Betty would be sad at the prospect of facing another Valentine's Day alone and not prioritized. Thus, priorly arranged arrangements were rearranged and Frank soon found himself with a ticket in hand for a magic carpet ride to visit God's country, a place he had never really seen in this life, but that he was partial to, as every iteration of her that he had ever known hailed from there. Frank made these plans without consulting with Betty and without even knowing if she would want to see him. He did it out of the feelings he had for her.

As a writer at heart, Frank lived in his head and was prone to conjuring up wildly romantic stories. To do so, however, Frank needed to quiet his mind and get in touch with his creative side. Living inspired allowed him to easily do that. So did airports, for airports always held the promise of new places and new people or of returning home to familiar places and familiar people, both scenarios being conducive to magic in Frank's mind. As he sat in the terminal waiting to board the magic carpet, not knowing what the next two days would be like, Frank easily conjured up in his mind what he hoped the next two days would bring. He could readily visualize this because he had lived those two days before. Not in another life or in a parallel universe with Betty, but rather in this life and with someone other than Betty.

At one point in his past, while learning to perform his magic in a long island in the Empire State, Frank had felt homesick and lonely one Christmas season, as he was not able to go home to visit his family. Frank had noticed her before, always sitting at the front of the class, her blonde hair pulling his gaze away from the many professorial dissertations that he was expected to endure, so as to have certain important knowledge imparted onto him. This day was the last day of the semester and Frank knew he would have to withstand another holiday season away from his family—alone and lonely. In his heart, Frank was not sure that she was her, but he felt compelled to speak to her nonetheless, out of a combination of longing and loneliness.

She was open to his opening gambit, and they soon met for coffee during the Christmas break and many times after that. Frank soon realized that she was innocent besides being young. This suited him fine, as he was searching most of all for a companion and a friend in her. Soon their friendship grew, and eventually she felt the desire to offer Frank a most special gift. Frank did not want to take the gift, as he felt undeserving, but she insisted, saying she yearned to know. By this time in their relationship, Frank's feelings for her had not yet reached the intensity where he would have felt comfortable accepting such a special treasure.

Frank always saw himself as an honorable man and always tried to do the right thing, so he refused the gift, telling her he felt it was not his to have. She appealed to his sense of friendship and his giving nature and eventually convinced him to take it, an act he has felt ambivalent about ever since. Besides the enduring guilt for taking that which was not meant for him, Frank was also left with a perpetual sense of responsibility toward her. To this day, whenever he visits the long island in the Empire State, Frank feels compelled to reach out and see how she is getting along.

On one particular visit to the long island years ago, Frank reached out to her while he was driving in her direction, as it was on the way to where he was staying. Frank knew that she was engaged and would soon be married. She had told him so during his phone call the prior year. He had been joyful for her when he heard the news. She was extremely happy herself, as things for her were going swimmingly, until they weren't.

When Frank called that day, she promptly answered in a state of panic. Several days prior, while making plans for her wedding, the bride and groom's respective families, which were from different cultures, had collided in a bad way, leaving the soon-to-be-married couple unsure as to whether they wanted to continue with their nuptial plans. The disagreement had to do with the religious education of the potential future offspring of the now-not-so-happy couple. This was just one of the many ways that the underlying issue could manifest itself, as the possibilities were endless.

Frank understood her predicament and his heart went out to her. He was keenly aware that sometimes

God played these tricks of granting our most ardent prayers but sent them in the wrong gift boxes. Frank knew that as human beings, we are all born with or eventually learn certain preferences and biases that are beyond our control, and are exacerbated when we come in close contact with others who are different than us. Sometimes these biases are veiled even from ourselves, but are nonetheless present. As he had gotten a bit older, Frank had begun to understand this more. His hope was that the love between his friend and her beloved was of such strength as to be able to bridge this cultural gap that existed between their families and perhaps even between themselves. His ardent hope for himself was that if he ever found "her," the same would hold true: that he and his beloved would be able to overcome any potential gaps between them.

Frank felt terrible upon hearing the news and tried all he could to console his friend. He talked to her about their past, about their long friendship, about her future, and about how he was sure that this crisis would soon pass. Frank told his friend that she would soon be made whole again. She continued to be despondent and did not share his optimism, as she and her fiancé had officially terminated their relationship days prior. Their conversation continued as Frank drove further west; he soon realized he would be driving close to where his friend lived.

In this life, Frank had been born a provider and a protector. As he drove west that day, he had in his possession nourishment which he had procured by his own hand on the east end of that long island in the Empire State. Talking on the phone that day, Frank felt very protective of his friend. He felt compelled to help her. At some point in the conversation, she told him that all she wished for at that moment was that he was there with her so that she could see him once again and touch him. She told him that she wanted him to hold her, as she had always found great comfort in their friendship and his embrace. Frank immediately felt himself inspired and saw all possibilities. He knew instantly what needed to be done.

After a few more minutes of talking, Frank gently asked his friend if she would be willing to play a game with him. He assured her that playing the game would make her feel better. She tentatively agreed, her sobbing clearly evident as she spoke. Frank told her to, right then and there, close her eyes and imagine that he now stood outside her door. She did. After several seconds, he asked her to now open her eyes and slowly walk toward the door, imagining with every step the increasing possibility of him being there. She did. He directed her to just walk to the door, but not to open it. Frank told her that if she really believed it with all her heart, he would be standing on the opposite side of the threshold as per her wishes. Frank then asked his friend to open the door. She did, and he was. This event had always been one of Frank's fondest memories, and one of those precious moments that he felt made his life worth living.

Frank's friend prepared the nourishment that he had brought for them while he showered. They ate it accompanied with red wine and talked all the while. Upon finishing dinner, she asked Frank if he would stay the night and comfort her. Frank agreed. She asked him to please hold her. He lovingly complied and did so for the entire night, as she slept peacefully in his arms with her head on his shoulder. Frank did not sleep that night, savoring the moment in his life when he first became aware of his true destiny, to be of service to those he loved. That awesome epiphany made him extremely happy. It made him feel whole, needed—useful. Frank always considered that night as one of the cherished-few seminal events of his life.

While sitting at the airport, listening to the music popular in God's country and waiting to board the magic carpet, Frank relived that night in the long island in the Empire State in his mind time and time again. Suddenly, Frank felt a sense of purpose. That prior episode had taken place by happenstance; now he felt as though he had been called to create a similar one just as special, perhaps even more so. The first episode had taken place without any effort or planning on his part. If he were to repeat it, he would have to make it happen by prioritizing Betty to a high degree. He would have to will it to happen. Like turbulent waters flow down a riverbed upon the rupture of a dam, random thoughts rushed into Frank's mind simultaneously. Spontaneously, these thoughts coalesced into a plan of action.

Frank then felt compelled to pull the magic tablet he had in his travel bag and begin to write. The words flowed from him like the sweat that poured out of his body after a long run. Like the tears that fell from his eyes the only two times in his life he remembers crying: the day each of his parents died. He wrote while waiting to board, and while on the magic carpet ride to his destination. He thought about what he would write next as he rented a carriage and pointed it northwest, toward God's country. He drove with purpose toward the town named after someone, located halfway between here and there. Frank wrote all that day and all that night. The story was inside him and he felt compelled to get it out. He then had the sudden realization that he was not really composing a story; rather, he was transcribing it. Almost as if the story had already been written and its ending was preordained. The words poured out of him until they didn't—the only part left unfinished being the ending.

The morning of Valentine's Day, Frank woke up early as usual. He knew the day would be cold and he confirmed it by looking out the hotel room window. A light snow was falling and would fall all day. Frank remembered Betty did not like the cold. This would not start as a good day for her. If he had anything to do with it, he would make sure the day ended on a better note. He looked across the parking lot outside his window and saw the restaurant where he hoped he would dine with Betty that evening. The restaurant named after another city in a town named after someone where Betty often ate with her relatives during family functions.

That morning, he planned to go for a ride. Frank would drive out to Indian Lake, about one hour away from the town named after someone where he was staying. He already felt her pull and felt close to her, sensing her presence not too far away. He wanted to gaze at the same familiar places that Betty had looked upon her entire life. He wanted to feel her presence in those places and smell her fragrance in the wind. He would then return to his hotel room to finish writing his story, as the only thing missing was the ending, which he did not yet know. He would get it ready and give it to her as a gift on that special night. Now it was time to put his plan into effect. Frank texted Betty that he missed her and that he truly hoped she could be with him that day. Full of hope and optimism, Frank showered, dressed, got into his rented carriage, and drove northwest.

Frank felt her pull from miles away. He knew that the way to Indian Lake would take him by her town and her parents' house, where Betty was staying. He then thought about what had happened to him driving that one night west on the long island in the Empire State. As he found himself driving northwest in God's country, he knew there was a chance the situation would repeat itself. As a matter of fact, he was convinced that in many universes parallel to this one, it was being repeated. The only question was, would it be repeated in this universe, at this time, in this life? He thought about what he would do if Betty called him at that instant and told him that she wanted to see him and have him hold her. Frank wondered whether he would do the same as he had done once before in that long island in the Empire State many years ago. Go running to her, go to her rescue. Frank would have done it in a heartbeat, but some concerns that he knew Betty harbored made him doubt as to whether he should.

As he got closer to her town, he feared that he did not know what he would do if indeed that call came. However, the call did not come, relieving Frank of the burden of having to make that difficult decision. He summoned all his strength not to get off the highway in what he knew was the exit to her parents' house on the west side of town. Betty's pull on him was strong, as it had always been. But he had promised her he would not do such a thing, that he would give her all the time and space she had requested. Besides, Frank knew Betty could not bring him to meet her parents or even talk to them about him. She did not think her parents would understand. Betty told him so the fifth night of their time together when Frank asked her casually how her parents were doing, after he heard her talking to them on the phone as he got dressed. Betty told Frank without hesitation, almost as if she had been thinking about it the entire day, that her parents were fine but that there was no way she could ever tell them about him, as they would never be able to understand. She told him so as they crossed Fifth Street in the tropical city by the sea, while on their way to the restaurant adjacent to the marina. That night was the night Betty told Frank that she had decided to leave and offered all her excuses, not realizing that she had already unknowingly divulged the real reason why.

God had indeed played a trick on them. He had made Frank and Betty inseparable and kindred spirits to stay together throughout all of eternity, but as an afterthought, God threw in a twist at the last minute. Although he allowed Frank and Betty to always be born in the same era, he had them born somewhat apart in time, where Frank always ended up being a bit older than she. At times where there were not many others in the world or where they had found each other in nearly deserted islands or sparsely populated lands, this had never been an issue. However, when they found each other at a time when there were plenty of people around, their age gap had always been an issue—a big issue, as most times it is hard not to be affected or influenced by the opinion of others, particularly those who happen to be family and friends. A significant age difference between lovers is one of those things, most times with good justification, that is not readily accepted nor easily tolerated by the relatives and friends of the lovers involved.

Frank had been mad at God for playing this cruel trick on them as it more times than not led to them not being together. Sometimes it was Frank who felt guilty and unworthy of being with her, pretty much the way he had felt accepting that special gift that did not belong to him. Most times, however, it was Betty who could not stand the pressure and the thought of the guaranteed disapproval that she was sure she would receive from her parents and relatives upon hearing the news of Frank and her. The thought of her parents' disapproval was unbearable to her. Frank understood as in this particular situation, God had assigned Betty the heavier burden.

In this life, Betty had been born with the nature to please others, and loving her parents the way she did, it was them whom she wished to please the most. Not recognizing Frank for who he really was, it was easy for her to leave him the moment she realized that having him was incompatible with having the approval of her parents, whom she loved very much. Being of a giving nature, it was easy for Betty to let go of Frank, no matter how good he made her feel or how much attraction she felt toward him. Frank's failure to make Betty remember who he was made it easier for her to leave. Frank understood her leaving and quietly reprimanded himself for failing at getting her to remember who he was—who they were.

At one point many lifetimes ago, Frank had, out of anger, appealed to God to reverse his original decision. The request was not granted. Eventually, Frank came to understand that God had not played this trick on them out of malice or some form of punishment, but rather as a testament to the love God thought possible for the two of them. God did it as a testament to who he thought Frank and Betty were—to who he *knew* Frank and Betty were—for they were his creation.

God knew that the love Frank felt for Betty was so strong that he would be driven to do anything he could to consummate it. He also knew that once Betty recognized Frank for who he was, she would do the same. God, as a testament to the potential of what their love could be, threw a challenge into the mix. For them to be together, their love would have to be of such strength as to overcome that significant hurdle that God had put in their paths. Most times, they tried and failed, but in some lives and at certain times, they had managed to overcome. The resulting love they shared felt like they were drinking the nectar from the sweetest fruits found in heaven.

In this life and in every other life, Frank had been born a human and not perfect. Although he knew God's reasoning, he would still not understand nor accept it. He continued to appeal to God to please take away the challenge and let Betty and him fulfill their destiny unmolested. God's mind would not be changed by Frank's pleas, but he did feel compelled to intervene. God conjured a wise butterfly spirit and sent it to deliver a message to Betty. The message was delivered in the form of sage grandmotherly advice. Betty jokingly told her grandmother one day that she might have feelings for someone whom Betty assumed her grandmother wouldn't approve of. To Betty's surprise, her grandmother was very accepting of her alleged beloved and told Betty that if she loved him, he would be welcomed into their family.

Frank had instantly recognized God's intervention the moment Betty told him that story. But she failed to recognize it as such, just as she had failed to recognize him for who he really was. Being older than Betty, Frank was also a bit wiser. He thought perhaps he could share some helpful advice of his own. He thought he could tell her how everyone was worth the benefit of the doubt, and that if she were to bring up Frank to her parents in the right context, maybe they too would surprise her. Perhaps they would at least agree to meet him before making a final judgment as to his suitability as a suitor for Betty. Frank felt that upon meeting him and realizing how he felt for their daughter, they would be able to find it within their hearts to accept him into their family. The way they had done so many times before, in so many different lives, where a similar situation had unfolded. Frank always loved the salt-of-the-earth people who hailed from God's country, because they had always accepted him. Whatever permutation of him they encountered, they had always taken him in, offered him shelter, offered him their warmth and caring friendship. They had always accepted him for who he was, as they could tell that his heart was pure and devoid of cruelty.

Frank then thought better of it. Suggesting that type of advice unsolicited was never a good idea, for if Betty followed it and the results were not as they hoped, Betty would resent him for it and their friendship would end. The last thing that Frank wanted was to possibly do anything that would cause his friendship with Betty to end. The thought of being the reason for a potential conflict between Betty and her parents was unthinkable.

Thus, Frank found himself in a confounding conundrum. He had advice and wisdom to share with Betty but could not do so until Betty requested it of him. He then thought about all the conversations he wanted to have with her in the tropical city by the sea. How he wanted to tell her of all the wisdom and gifts he had collected over the years and saved for her, how he could not wait to give them to her. Then he thought how, in a similar way, gifts that were not welcomed and would not be accepted in good faith should never be offered. Frank then realized that although it was his job to lovingly woo Betty, if she did not surrender herself to him willingly, he did not have a right to take her love in this life nor in any other. God had put forth a challenge for them as a couple, but yet another one for him as an individual. In each and every life and every time he was lucky enough to find her, Frank had been challenged with making Betty remember who he was, making Betty remember who they were. This was the prerequisite without which their eternal love for one another could not be realized.

Driving his carriage while lost in his thoughts as he was, Frank soon found himself at Indian Lake. He had never seen it before but now he would not be lying to Betty if he ever told her that he had been there previously. He reveled in having had a chance to look with his own eyes at places that Betty had looked upon all her life. He still felt the gravitational pull of being close to her, but now the pull was much deeper, more primal, almost reptilian in nature. Now, having visited God's country, where God's salt-of-the-earth people hail from, he felt he had gotten to know her better—gotten yet that much closer to her spirit, to her eternal essence.

Frank drove back to the town named after someone, located halfway between here and there. He reached his hotel shortly after noon. Frank did not feel hungry and knew that day he would not eat. There was no way that he could, due to the intensity of the emotions twirling through him. He had heard from Betty via text while driving back, and she had told him that she missed him too and wished that she would be spending that day and evening with him. Betty freely volunteered that she had been feeling gloomy for the last several days, the feeling becoming more intense on that particular morning, as she once again found herself alone on Valentine's Day. Frank felt incredibly optimistic upon reading this and would soon put his plan into effect.

One of the gifts that Frank had sent to Betty via carrier pigeon days prior was a note with an invite for Betty to accompany him to the last island at the end of the overseas highway, where arrangements had been arranged for them to have Valentine's Day dinner at his favorite restaurant there. In the note, Frank informed Betty that he planned to go on the trip either way, whether she accompanied him or not.

Now back at his hotel room, Frank texted Betty and asked her if she would be willing to play a game with him—a game that he knew would make her feel much better. Once she replied in the affirmative as he hoped, Frank would then be able to compose the end of the story he was writing, place it in the pink gift box he had brought for the occasion, and bring it to Betty as a gift when he saw her that evening, as he expected he would.

Upon Betty agreeing to play the game with him, Frank would then text that he felt terribly alone sitting at the island at the end of the overseas highway and that he missed her. That the tourist season there was light this year and that his favorite restaurant would be able to seat him at whatever time he pleased. He would ask her when she might be able to find some time for him that night. He would tell her that he had once seen this romantic movie where two lovers were in a similar situation and had decided to play a most unique game of eating together, alone.

Frank would explain to Betty that the basic idea was to have dinner or at least a coffee at the same time in different restaurants in the cities where the lovers found themselves, but while doing so, talk on the phone as if they were sitting across from one another. Frank would also tell Betty that he would like to suggest the restaurant she should go to. Upon Betty agreeing, Frank would remind Betty of a college friend he had mentioned to her previously, who had attended law school in a town not too far from God's country.

Frank would then tell Betty that his friend Rio had an acquaintance in school who owned a cabin at a place called Indian Lake, not too far from where Rio lived at the time and the town where Frank knew her parents' house was located. Rio would often take Frank there whenever Frank came to visit, so that they could go fishing. On their drive there and back, they stopped along the way at a particular restaurant named after another city, in a town named after someone, located halfway between here and there. Frank would tell Betty that he always felt at home there eating with his friend and thus, had a deep attachment to that particular eatery. Thinking of it reminded him of happy times during his college years. Frank would then ask Betty if she would be willing to go there and play with him the game of eating together, alone.

Frank knew that Betty would think his restaurant suggestion odd, as it was the place where she and her relatives got together on a regular basis for family dinners. Even if Betty remembered mentioning this establishment to Frank months prior, she had only done so in passing and had never mentioned the restaurant by name. Thus, she would not be suspicious as to why Frank would suggest it and would think of it most likely as a most unlikely coincidence. It was the opening gambit of this plan that Frank texted Betty and for which he now waited on a response. He had asked her if she would be willing to play a game with him, a game that was sure to make her feel better and lift both their moods.

Despite being happy in the land that protrudes into the sea, Betty had willingly returned to God's country where it was cold because she felt that her family needed her. Upon receiving the text from Frank, Betty thought that it would be nice to play a game; it would perhaps take her mind away temporarily and brighten her mood. However, that day she had already made a commitment to please her family.

Frank's attention was drawn from the window upon hearing the unmistakable sound of a text coming through on his phone. He walked over to the desk where his phone sat next to his magic tablet and read the message. Betty's disappointing answer was always a possibility in Frank's mind, but reading it made it suddenly real; it momentarily took his breath away, and not in a good way. Betty had politely declined his offer and explained the reason why. Not wanting to hurt him, she added that perhaps they could text or talk later on that evening. He replied like he always did, telling her that it was okay, that he understood. He reminded her that Frank and Betty were, had always been, and would always be good.

It turned out that Betty had already made plans to babysit her two sisters' children that night, so her sisters could go to Valentine's Day dinner with their significant others. The disappointing news caused

Frank to lose his balance, and he braced himself by sitting on the chair by the desk. Then it all became clear to him. As the proposed proposal for cognitive consideration had not borne fruit, he was only left with the acceptable alternative, which he had also considered days before, as he pondered future possibilities. Frank now knew how the story he was writing would end.

Frank straightened himself on the chair by the desk, faced the magic tablet with the unfinished story still showing on the screen as he had left it earlier, and commenced writing. The words flowed out of him like the sweat from his body after a long run. Like the tears flowed from his eyes the only three times in his life that he had cried. The words kept coming and coming until there were no other words left to write. The story he had been writing was finally finished. Once it was put to writing, it felt as if a piece had been torn out of his heart, which, rather than belonging to him, had always been meant as a gift for Betty.

God expected a busy day as he always did on special occasions like Valentine's Day. On these days, the prayers and appeals increased exponentially. Lost souls appealed for guidance, for a second chance, for a kindred companion, for someone who would prioritize them in their lives—prioritize them on this night—for hope…for love. God visualized these prayers as points of lights directed to him from the eternity of time, all across this universe and the many universes that he had created. That day, the prayers had come in droves as expected. They came in fast and strong, like the waters would flow down riverbeds if an infinite number of dams gave way simultaneously. That night, God noted a light that shone brighter than a thousand others. It was coming from this universe, from this time, from this life. It appeared to move. As God took a closer look, he realized that it was moving slowly across a parking lot toward a restaurant named after another city, in a town named after someone, halfway between here and there.

God immediately knew it was Frank, as he always remembered this creation of his, an audacious human who had questioned God's wisdom many times throughout the ages. Frank had questioned why he had been sent a precious treasure in the wrong gift box and had pleaded with God to place the gift in a more suitable wrapping. Frank's hubris was not well received—nor was his current audacity in thinking he could recreate a special moment that had been facilitated for him years prior, so that he could learn his true destiny, the reason he had been born. God felt that he had taught this impertinent human yet another lesson this time, but nonetheless felt sorry for him. Frank's light shone extremely bright, and God knew the reason why. It was the love Frank held in his heart. God felt sorry for Frank and decided to bestow upon him a very special gift. Frank was allowed a vision of a parallel universe and the events taking place there on that day.

After stepping out into the cold, snowy night, Frank had directed his footsteps toward the restaurant named after another city, located in a town named after someone. His footsteps on the snow would soon be covered by new snow, but the energy that he radiated was so strong that it would leave an indelible mark in that place throughout all eternity. Frank knew that it was a long shot for his scheme to have succeeded. He had attempted to recreate a moment in his life that he had been gifted so that he could know his true destiny and the reason why he existed. Frank now understood that trying to recreate that moment was not his role in this life. Rather, it was his role to experience it, feel it, and if so moved, live it. But Frank, because he was living inspired at the time he conceived of his plan, also was aware of the possibility of failure and had formulated an acceptable alternative that he was now putting into effect.

Frank purposefully walked across the parking lot toward the restaurant named after another city, in a town named after someone, located halfway between here and there. In his hands, he was holding a pink box containing the story he had written, which was meant for Betty. It was her Valentine's Day gift. As he approached the restaurant door, he dared ponder what he would have felt knowing that Betty was sitting inside, talking to him on the phone, playing his concocted game of eating together, alone. He could easily imagine the celestial smile that would have appeared on her face if, upon raising her eyes from her phone, Betty saw him materialize for her, standing right in front of the table where she sat. As his mind visualized the possibility of that reality (perhaps in another life, in another time, in another parallel universe), Frank's eternal light shone so bright that even God could not help but notice the exponential increase in intensity. As Frank touched the restaurant's front door to open it so that he could step inside, he received his gift. He was allowed the vision of a parallel universe. In his mind's eye, Frank was able to see the events taking place there at that exact moment in time.

CHAPTER 2

Jay and Kelly

In this vision Frank and Betty were Jay and Kelly. Jay was relaxing in the pool just outside bungalow eighteen at his favorite hotel, in his favorite island at the end of the overseas highway. He liked going to that spot, as he felt peaceful there. It was a place where he always found God, whether he went looking for him or not. On this day, Jay was extremely happy as he knew inside bungalow eighteen, Kelly was getting ready so that they could go to Valentine's Day dinner later that evening. He knew that soon she would be out of the bathroom and would call for him to come out of the pool and get ready. While he waited, Jay thought about the strange sequence of events that began with him answering her siren call and ended with him being there with her. As he waited, Jay lay his head back and closed his eyes. His arms were spread wide as he held onto the pool edge on which his head rested. His body floated in the warm water. Jay let his mind wander freely, feeling himself fully alive in that moment, in that place, in this life, as he waited to hear her angelic voice, which would soon be calling out to him.

Kelly was happy to have come from God's country, where the salt-of-the-earth people hailed from. She had never traveled far from home; in fact, she had not traveled much at all in part due to some challenges that she had experienced with her health as a young woman right out of college. The health issues had mostly been resolved, but she was left with the scars—physical and psychological—to remind her daily of that time in her life. Kelly had been born in this life tall, strong, and athletic. Her health issues had been unexpected, scary, and psychologically traumatic. They had made her mature beyond her years. Kelly had told herself that her health challenges were a gift from God to bring her down a peg, to make her more appreciative of the gifts she had been granted—to humanize her. Yet as human, flawed, and not perfect, at times Kelly was less than happy with God for having put that challenge in her life.

As a result of her health issues, Kelly had gotten progressively less fond of the cold weather. She loved God's country, but when it got cold there, her mood changed, her outlook became less bright, and her body ached when she arose in the morning. As a child, she had visited the land that protrudes into the sea, as Gramps at one point owned a house there. Kelly loved going to visit Gramps; she had come to love it more and more as she grew older, as in that part of the country the weather was warm year-round.

Over the past couple of years, Kelly had toyed with the idea of moving south somewhere with warmer weather. She was sad that moving would take her away from her family, whom she loved very much, but she explained that it was for the betterment of her health, physical and otherwise, and they understood. Kelly began the process of planning an extended trip to the land that protrudes into the sea so that she could see how living there would suit her. As she did so, out of impulse one day, she put out a siren call. After all, she needed to practice her flirting skills so as to be ready for the day when and if "he" came. She had been waiting for him her entire life and had grown weary and impatient with the passing years, as he had not yet materialized.

One fine day while Kelly was engaged in her daily toil, her siren call was answered. She was intrigued about the peculiar manner in which it had been answered, as his was different than any other mating call she had heard before. The tones of it, the way he expressed himself, left her curious and wanting to learn more.

Kelly had already made one big mistake in her life and had promised to herself she would not repeat it. In this life, Kelly always knew exactly the type of dog she wanted. It would not be one of those ankle-biters, particularly not the smaller variety that tended to look like rabbits. No, she wanted a larger, well-groomed, well-mannered dog. Then one day, she was asked to temporarily tend to a discarded dog by the name of Mildred, for whom a home was being sought. Mildred was four and a half years old, already had some concerning habits, and had the blood and instincts of a hunting dog. Mildred was nice and friendly once she became familiar with someone, but she was not necessarily that well-behaved overall, as there was a wild side to her likely to come out unexpectedly at any time. However, after spending time with Mildred, Kelly began to feel drawn to her. What happened next was utterly unexpected and formed a grip on Kelly's heart that has grown ever since and has a hold on her to this day.

Kelly fell in love with Mildred and soon realized that she could not part with her. She decided to adopt Mildred and become a dog mom. Mildred changed Kelly's life profoundly, in ways that she could never have anticipated. Although happy with her decision regarding Mildred, Kelly swore to herself that she would never allow something similar to happen to her again. She would never allow anything or anyone to sneak up on her heart in the same way. In the future, Kelly would inspect gifts she was offered, starting with the box they were wrapped in. She would not allow her heart to leap until she was absolutely sure that it was the gift she wanted, that it was him, the one exclusively meant for her. Kelly had always told herself that the man she was waiting for would be perfect, that everything about him would be as it should be, including the package he was wrapped in.

However, the call that was answering hers was intriguing. Some unique tones contained therein were such that it seemed as if only her ears could hear them. The peculiar way in which he expressed himself seemed uniquely catered to her. She felt intrigued, curious, drawn. Once further bonding occurred, Kelly felt a need to share more. And so, she did. She told her potential suitor about herself, her challenges, her plans, and her hopes. She felt the need to keep a connection with him, to regularly be in touch with him. Her potential suitor showed interest, listened, expressed concern for her safety, metaphorically walked beside her. Kelly did not intend for this to happen, but being born in this life as a hopeless romantic, she allowed her mind to consider the possibilities. She cautiously gave free reign to her imagination. Kelly allowed her heart to spread its wings and fly, albeit only for short, cautious sprints.

As the days grew closer for her planned departure to the land that protrudes into the sea, Kelly became increasingly excited about her trip and the possibilities it portended. She knew that as she traveled south and away from God's country, she would eventually come to a fork in the road. To the right awaited her well-laid plans, the volleyball house with the great scene there, old and new friends. To the left awaited the unknown, possibilities, and him, her potential suitor who had answered her siren call with the most unique call of his own. By this time, Kelly had entertained her potential suitor's invite to the tropical city by the sea, so that they could meet. The idea of meeting him intrigued and excited her to the point that she had, with some reservations and after considerable contemplation, accepted his invite for a visit. As she drove south, she felt a need to talk to him and be close to him. He in turn responded to her every call and spoke of lifelong friendship, kindred spirits, and his desire to meet her. Kelly, being born in this life as responsible and sensible, took a hold of her heart and, preventing it from leaping, told herself that this was an adventure, nothing more.

While driving south, shortly before coming to the fork in the road, while in conversation with her potential suitor, Kelly had the sudden realization that there was something about Jay that she did not like. This epiphany caught her by surprise. Jay's age had been obvious all along as Jay had never lied or deceived her about it, but somehow, she had consciously or subconsciously failed to cognitively internalize this particular fact about him. Jay, in turn, was just as surprised at her surprise and could not believe she did not know that part of him, as he had been up front about that information all along. Jay had prominently displayed his imperfections, as Kelly had innocently displayed hers.

This realization occurred just as Kelly was approaching the fork in the road, and Jay gave her the option to take the road to the right, which led to her well-laid plans, the volleyball house, and the great scene there in the balmy city by the gulf. Jay assured Kelly that it would be okay if she chose this option as he understood, and besides, no harm or foul had been done. In a fraction of a second, Kelly pondered and decided that she would take the left fork in the road, the one that led to the tropical city by the sea that by now, in her mind, was less full of possibilities, as her suitor was now less suitable. Alas, by then she was committed. By then she was trapped.

Then they met. Jay seemed friendly and welcoming enough, but Kelly felt ambivalent. She was nervous, but at the same time somehow felt at ease. Kelly felt that Jay could be trusted, relied upon, allowed in—but only to a certain extent, as by now she knew that he had been sent to her in the wrong gift box. She instinctively knew that Jay would not harm her. Jay was no longer a suitable suitor in Kelly's eyes, but looking at the gift at face value, she was not displeased. He was pleasant of form and character. Moreover, Kelly realized that particularly at a certain distance, looking at him from certain angles and if the light hit him just right, Jay could have been thought of as handsome.

Jay held the door open to his abode in the sky and welcomed Kelly and Mildred. Upon entering, Kelly was pleased to see the apartment was kept immaculately clean and orderly. It faced west and was on the heaventh floor of a building immediately adjacent to the bay. As soon as Kelly stepped over the threshold, she could see the calm waters of the bay right outside the balcony window, immaculate islands with beautiful homes beyond, and the skyline of the tropical city by the sea beyond that. Kelly had arrived after dark. The view that awaited her as she entered was heavenly. It was the kind of scene that is conducive for the mind to wander into the land of dreams.

Thus, it was with this initial introduction that Kelly eagerly undertook to her adventure. After all, her illness had robbed her of her twenties, and she had missed plenty of adventures that are part and parcel of being young. She was due some, and she was committed to partake of this one. Kelly sensed that Jay was struggling with a promise he had made her as a condition of her visit. As she knew that Jay wouldn't harm her, Kelly engaged in friendly, flirtatious banter and geographical exploration. She teased him and was glad to see that at times, he was powerless to resist her charms.

Over the next three days, Kelly and Jay spent a lot of quality time together after work. They spent this time walking Mildred, eating, talking, and drinking wine. During their dinners, Kelly talked incessantly as Jay listened captivated, mesmerized. On the day of the fourth night, Jay texted Kelly that he would be having dinner with his sister, and he would love for her to join. Kelly was nervous about this invite as she did not necessarily want to meet his family, fearing that would complicate things. She wanted to keep this adventure to just the two of them. But as the day wore on, Kelly became intrigued about the invitation and started to get ready to go to dinner. However, she struggled with her hair and could not get it exactly right. Frustrated, Kelly began to second-guess her decision and eventually decided not to go. Kelly texted Jay that she was going to stay home and use the opportunity to read the two chapters out of his manuscript, which the day before he had printed and placed on her nightstand. He had previously sent her those two chapters via text message, but she could not read them as the print was too small on her phone. Jay had shared these two chapters as they spoke of him, of his nature.

The fourth night that they spent together was the first time that Kelly got to know Jay in a deeper sense.

The chapters he had given her spoke of his passion for his vocation and of his ability to love. After reading these chapters, she felt for the first time that he was real, that he really existed. Kelly had gotten a hint by now as to Jay's overall demeanor, but in the time spent together, she had done most—if not all—the talking while Jay patiently listened, as if what she had to say were the most insightful observations known to man. However, by his ways, his actions, and the way he treated her and Mildred, Kelly was already getting an idea as to Jay's personality and temperament. Reading the two chapters gave Kelly a deeper insight and appreciation as to Jay's true nature and way of thinking. She felt kind of sad about it, because Jay had been given to her inside the wrong gift box, making him not suitable as a suitor.

Jay eventually came home and brought Kelly nourishment, which he had procured by the fruits of his labor. She ate it while they drank wine and talked. That night, Kelly felt exponentially closer to him than she had the previous three nights, perhaps because she had gotten to know him at a deeper level after reading the two chapters. Strangely, Kelly felt a need to be as physically close to Jay as possible; she cuddled up to him as they spoke. As she listened, Kelly became aware of an unfamiliar emotion swelling up deep inside her. Suddenly, something stirred in her heart. Kelly was overcome by the feeling that she had experienced this closeness to Jay before, almost as if she had previously lived this moment. She felt as if somehow they had crossed paths before, perhaps in her imagination, or perhaps in one of her dreams. As they talked, this feeling exponentially grew in intensity and eventually overwhelmed her with a strange mixture of excitement, joy, and fear. Almost as if in a state of panic, Kelly felt the need to stop further interaction with Jay at that moment and proclaimed she was tired and wanted to turn in. Kelly found it hard to fall asleep that night, as her mind was in turmoil, incessantly searching for a long-forgotten memory that was just beyond her reach.

The morning of the fifth day, Kelly woke up scared. Her mood had been volatile for a couple of days but upon awakening that morning, she felt a deep sense of gloom. Jay was as loving in his ways as always but once he left for work, fear started to creep into Kelly's heart. Doubts arose in her mind like the corn grows in God's country during harvest season, fast and strong. Kelly tried to get her mind into the mundane tasks related to her work, but she could not. A certain fear crept into her as when one gets too close to a fire. At first its warmth feels good, especially when it's cold outside, but eventually one realizes the possibility of being consumed by that fire; the instinctive reaction is to get away from it, to run. Kelly started to sense that she had wandered onto unsafe ground. She feared she might be in trouble. The fear eventually overwhelmed her, and her immediate reaction was to run away. Thus, following the arc of every great love story ever lived, told, or conceived of, she set her mind to do just that.

Kelly had already made the mistake with Mildred of letting an unexpected gift, wrapped in the wrong gift box, sneak into her heart. She was not about to let that happen to her again. For the fraction of a second that Kelly allowed herself to contemplate the possibility that she might overlook the gift box that Jay came in, she mentally reprimanded herself. Her being with Jay in any way other than the adventure she was on was impossible. Her parents would not understand, her friends would not understand, the world would not understand. Kelly already had enough to deal with regarding the future geographical location she would end up in and with whom. She did not need added stress piled on. After thinking about it all day, Kelly made the decision that when Jay came home that night, she would tell him she was going to leave and go to the balmy city by the gulf, on the other side of the land that protrudes into the sea, where she had originally planned to go in the first place.

Jay came home the night of the fifth day full of energy and hope. Kelly could sense that in him, so she thought it was best to prepare him by telling him that she needed to discuss something after dinner. Jay showered, dressed, and took Kelly to the next restaurant that he wanted her to experience, an outdoor café adjacent to a marina, located within walking distance from where he lived. That night, Kelly did not sense any difference in Jay's behavior at first, but eventually she noted a bit of melancholy or perhaps some withdrawal or distraction on his part. Almost as if Jay was searching for something in his head while he sat there listening to her.

When they got back home, Kelly noticed that Jay behaved differently than usual in that he was not as engaging. When she suggested that they open a bottle of wine and go sit in the balcony, Jay told Kelly that he would be turning in early that night but would be happy to prepare a glass for her. She sensed the difference in Jay's demeanor and decided that this was the moment to tell him, and so she did. The excuses that Kelly heard coming from her mouth were as varied as they were untrue. She knew this, and she knew that Jay knew it too because he told her so. However, Kelly did not want to hurt Jay and did the best she could. The one thing that Kelly uttered that was true was that she did not want to hurt him and ruin his life like she had watched other women do to their men. To this pronouncement, Jay responded that although she could surely hurt him, she did not have the power to ruin his life. Only he held that power and he had not, nor would he ever, cede that power to her or anyone else. Jay told Kelly that it was he and he alone who held the sole responsibility for living his life and fulfilling his destiny, just like she held the sole responsibility for living and fulfilling hers.

Emotionally exhausted from the effort, Kelly eventually went to bed and drifted off to sleep. She was not aware of Jay until she woke up the next morning. Again, he was loving as always but not as warm, almost as if he was afraid to come close or touch her. Kelly stole a kiss from Jay that morning as he rode down on the elevator with her and Mildred, and then went off to work. Or so she thought.

While her elevator door was closing on her way back up from walking Mildred, Kelly saw the door open in the elevator across from hers and Jay walk out of it. Kelly was a bit confused, as she had just seen Jay walk to his car minutes prior when they had gone down in the elevator together. Perplexed, Kelly inquired as to what Jay was doing. He muttered something that she could not hear, as by then her elevator door was almost completely closed. When she got up to the apartment, Kelly learned what Jay had been doing. On her nightstand, there was an envelope with Jay's last effort to get her to stay.

One of Kelly's excuses for leaving was that she felt bad staying at his place because she had made a mess of it with all her travel things. In the note Jay wrote her, he told her that if that was really the issue, she could, for a couple of weeks, get a temporary place of her own close to him, rather than leave to the balmy city by the gulf on the opposite side of the land that protrudes into the sea, hours away from where he lived. In the envelope with the note, Jay had placed the funds necessary to make that possibility a reality. She felt bad for using that excuse, as she knew that Jay knew it for what it was. Kelly very much appreciated Jay's effort, however. She told him so. She texted him that he was an amazing man, and she meant it. She felt sad that Jay had been sent to her wrapped in the wrong gift box. She felt sad for him; she felt sad for herself. Kelly felt sad for them both.

Kelly was conflicted that day and tried to figure out when to leave. When she expressed ambivalence about leaving, and texted Jay that she was torn, Jay told her that if her mind was made up, then he thought she should leave. He felt that was the only chance he had of having her come back to him. Kelly then decided to be strong and do what needed to be done. She packed all her things and waited for Jay to come home.

While Kelly waited for Jay, she thought about this strange man who had come to her in the wrong gift box. He spoke in a rather peculiar way, with odd phrases and sentence construction that made it seem as if he was someone from a different reality or perhaps a different time—almost as if he existed in a different realm, somehow. He often said that he spoke in songs and occasionally uttered phrases remarkably similar to the ones she had heard in the music popular in God's country, but distorted or changed in some way. He would also often make comments that did not make any sense at the time he said them, but would dawn on her hours, days, perhaps years later. Yes, Kelly thought, a strange man indeed. One who refers to a car as a carriage, an apartment as a castle, and a surgeon as a sculptor.

Since the time that Kelly and Jay bonded and developed a connection, Kelly remembered waking up to a text from Jay every morning. Kelly slept like a log and never woke up when the texts came in, which at times was exceedingly early in the morning. She often wondered why Jay was usually up that early, as she knew that he stayed up late, much later than she did. Jay's text messages were usually cryptic—for example, altered fragments of a song, or a changed title of a book or movie, but somehow related to something pertaining to what they were discussing or interacting about around that time. Sometimes it took her a day or two to see the connection and that always made her happy, as it made her feel that Jay was somewhat witty and clever, and that she was too for being able to decipher his utterances. Kelly had always found smart to be sexy.

Other than the morning texts she received from Jay, Kelly noted that he rarely texted spontaneously. However, every time she texted him, he seemed to answer almost immediately in a similar interestingly cryptic manner; whenever she called him, he always answered the phone or called her back without fail. This was curious to her, as she knew how busy Jay was with his occupation, which required significant time, effort, and concentration on his part. Jay's perpetual attentiveness always made Kelly feel special, prioritized.

When Jay got home on the sixth night, Kelly was working on the dining room table. He walked through the door and seemed friendly and loving enough, but he did not kiss her or come close to her. As he usually did upon arriving from work, Jay went to take a shower. When he was finished and dressed, he told Kelly that seeing all her things packed made him feel a deep sadness. However, he was happy that she was still there, so that he could see her one more time before she left.

Jay confessed to Kelly that he might need her help through this situation, as he was not used to it nor good at saying goodbye. Kelly felt protective of him; she helped him by holding firm and acting somewhat detached and aloof. Kelly and Jay walked Mildred together one last time. Afterward, Jay helped take her luggage to her car. Shortly after, Kelly was driving past Jay as he opened the gate to the garage. She half-smiled at him but did not hesitate. Kelly went past the garage gate, turned right and right again, and pointed her car in the direction of the balmy city by the gulf.

The morning of the seventh day, Kelly heard from Jay asking if she had made it safely to her destination.

She curtly texted him in the affirmative and had every intention of leaving it at that. Not too long after though, Kelly began to think about Jay and how great a host he had been to Mildred and her during their visit. She felt compelled to text him that she missed him. Jay answered in kind but did not extrapolate. The next day and the days after that, similar exchanges happened time and time again, all initiated by Kelly. Jay had promised Kelly that he would give her the time and space she had told him she needed. Nonetheless, Kelly was somewhat disappointed when Jay did not reach out more during those first few days. However, she understood; Kelly sensed that it was important to Jay that she learn he was the type of man who kept his promises, was honorable, and always tried to do the right thing.

With the passage of time, things progressed as expected and Kelly slowly began feeling better about her emotional state. Kelly was getting to the point that she was not missing Jay as much. After all, she was back at the volleyball house and there was a great scene there. One evening, while feeling particularly vulnerable, Kelly reached out to Jay, but he was out dining with his family, and they could not connect. She had gone to sleep early that evening and missed his return call upon finishing dinner, as he had promised. Kelly woke up the following morning intending to call Jay back, but somehow became distracted and failed to do so as by then she was feeling much stronger emotionally. She did not make the call to Jay that day nor the days that followed. As the weeks passed without further interaction, Kelly began to gain emotional fortitude to the point that thoughts about Jay became scarce, albeit always associated with faint tugs at her heart.

Then one fine day many weeks later, Kelly received an anonymous text that contained a picture of a pink box. The accompanying text explained that a regular customer of a local restaurant had left a package for her there with instructions to try to get it to her by Friday that week, which heralded the beginning of Valentine's Day weekend. When she inquired as to who had left the package, the person texting her said that he did not know the gentleman's name but did recognize him as a regular customer of the restaurant where he was employed as the manager.

Kelly was intrigued and concerned at the same time. Very few people knew where she was, and a package being left for her at a random restaurant in the balmy city by the gulf was highly unusual. Kelly wondered who might have done that, but somehow sensed that there was no evil intent associated with the pink package. Gracious, the box was pink, and everyone knows that pink is a harmless, friendly, romantic color. Upon further consideration, she surmised it might have been Jay, as he had promised her an autographed copy of his book as soon as it became available. During one of their text exchanges weeks prior, he let her know that he had finally finished the editing process, in no small part due to being inspired by her. Kelly had responded by telling Jay that she was proud of him.

The following day, Kelly could not concentrate on her work; her mind was focused on the pink box, who it could be from, and what it could potentially contain. She had settled on Jay as the culprit, but did not understand why he had chosen to get her the pink box in this most peculiar way. Jay could have easily called her and asked for the address of where she was staying and mailed it to her there. She would have gladly given Jay that information, as she never thought he was capable of hurting her in any way. Jay was harmless, as he had told her so and had even shown her written proof. Besides, she knew Jay to be honorable and devoid of any cruelty in his heart.

Finally, she could no longer contain her curiosity and decided to drive the hour it took to get to the restaurant to pick up her gift. Kelly made it to the establishment a mere five minutes before it closed. A woman cleaning the tables inquired as to what she wanted. When Kelly responded with her name and told her she was there to pick up a package that had been left for her, she was told to wait. The woman went into the back office and came back with a medium-sized box wrapped in pink paper and handed it to her. The box was way too big for any book. Kelly was just as perplexed as ever as to who had left it and as to what might be inside.

Kelly carried the box to her car and experienced yet another challenge: opening it. Taped to the front of the box was a white paper with typed, large, bold font, which included her full name and cell phone number as the top line and two other lines below it. The first line indicated that, if possible, the gift should get to her by that Friday. The second line instructed that the box should be discarded, unopened, by the last day in February if by that time she had not picked it up. The note was attached to the box with thick, clear tape that was extremely sturdy and difficult to tear. Eventually, she had to resort to using her car keys to cut the tape so that she could open the package. Nothing was going to keep Kelly out of that box, and crafty as she was, she eventually devised a way to open it.

The moment Kelly opened the pink box she knew who it was from, as she immediately recognized Jay's cologne. It was obvious he had handled the box and its contents. Kelly's attention was then drawn to the yellow rubber ball that was one of Mildred's toys. She remembered that on the night she left, she asked Jay to look under the furniture, as she was sure that Mildred had hidden some of her toys there. Jay had reached under the center table and the L-shaped couch in his living room and pulled out many of her toys, including this yellow ball that was now in the pink box. Had

Jay purposely kept the yellow ball behind? Had Mildred taken it back out of her toy box when Kelly was not looking and left it hidden there so that it could be later found? Kelly would never know for sure unless Jay confessed, but she had a strong feeling that Mildred was the culprit. Kelly knew that Mildred was a very smart dog.

The rest of the package contained several smaller boxes and a pink envelope, which was sure to contain a Valentine's Day card. Kelly perused the contents of the box while sitting in her car in the parking lot, but as it was already getting late, she decided to start heading home and finish this exploratory task there. Upon commencing her drive back, she called Jay. Kelly was happy to talk to Jay and started the conversation by thanking him for her gifts and by excusing herself for being distant the prior few weeks. Jay did not seem mad nor upset in any way, so Kelly proceeded to tell him how exciting her little adventure regarding the pink box had been.

When Kelly inquired as to why he had made it so difficult to open the box, Jay responded that it was because he wanted to eliminate the possibility that the carrier pigeons, who had been commissioned to take her the box, would be tempted to open it to see what was inside. Jay told Kelly that he had wrapped the box in such a way that if it had been opened, she would have been able to tell. But to confirm that the pink box had reached Kelly unopened as intended, Jay asked her to please tell him what she had found inside it.

Kelly proceeded to tell Jay about the things she had found in the box when she opened it in her car and perused through its contents. First there was Mildred's ball, a nice card, and then there were other gifts. They consisted of either things that Jay had mentioned in passing, or things she had told him she liked on those days she had spent with him. Kelly remembered when she first came to visit Jay in the tropical city by the sea, he had placed several items on the top drawer of what was to be her nightstand. Jay told Kelly that these were house-warming gifts for her. One of them was in a slick, rectangular, white box. Jay explained that not finding any pencils with his name on them, he had found this other pencil instead.

By the time Jay said this to her, Kelly had already bonded and connected with Jay enough to know a bit of his nature. She had noticed that Jay often spoke in riddles and parables. His phrases and sayings reminded Kelly of songs that she had heard and were popular in God's country, movies she had seen, or books she had read. It took her several days to figure out the reference about the pencil with his name on it; it had to do with a movie that Kelly had mentioned to Jay weeks before. However, she was intrigued as to why Jay had chosen to give her this type of pencil in particular and not any other. He then casually mentioned that the pencil was a pair to a magic tablet that he had commissioned specifically for her. Jay told her that the magic tablet was to have her name on it, and it would be hers if she wanted it.

When Kelly mentioned one day that she had gotten a great price on her ear pods so she could use her phone while driving and working, Jay affirmed that those ear pods would not work best with the magic tablet that he had commissioned and that she should have new ones, also specifically made for her and with her name on them. When one morning she mentioned that she liked the charging station that was on her nightstand because she could charge several of her devices simultaneously, Jay stated that she would have one. All these things that Jay said to her in passing she thought at first were the ramblings of a madman. When Kelly left several days later, none of these things had materialized except for the pencil, which she had carefully placed back in the white box and had left on the top drawer of her nightstand in the tropical city by the sea.

Now all these items that Jay mentioned had miraculously appeared inside the pink box, which had been left for her by a regular customer that frequented a certain restaurant in the balmy city by the gulf where she was staying for the winter. The best way Kelly could describe what she had received was to say it was a pink gift box full of kept promises.

Upon hearing all the items that Kelly had found in the box, Jay seemed disappointed and informed Kelly that if that was all she found, it meant that the carrier pigeons he had commissioned had let curiosity get the best of them and had opened the pink box. Kelly thought that Jay was again speaking in riddles or in songs and could not figure out what he was talking about, as she was sure the box had not been opened. Gosh, it had taken her several minutes to open it, and she was not trying to do it in such a way as to not leave trace of it. However, Jay insisted that the box had been opened. That is, unless she was able to find yet another item in the box that he had placed there. Because they were having this phone conversation while she was driving, Jay asked her to please only look for that item after she got home, as he did not want her to take her eyes off the road or stop by the side of the road since it was already nighttime.

In this life, Kelly had been born the sort of person who follows rules. As Jay requested that she not take her eyes off the road, Kelly knew that this was not only sensible, but in the land that protrudes into the sea, it was also the law. Thus, she would have to wait until she got home to open the box and find the hidden treasure that she now surmised Jay had cleverly hidden in it. All the way home, Kelly wondered what else she might find in the pink box. As she reveled in the mystery of it and felt the kind of anticipation that a child would upon finding a Christmas gift under the tree, she realized what a sweet adventure she had been sent on. Then it dawned on her that although this adventure was unique to her, she was aware of adventures like it. Not necessarily because she had previously lived them in this life or any other, but because she had seen them acted out in movies and television shows, or she had read about them in books. Kelly then remembered that she had previously told Jay what a hopeless romantic she was, and the kind of movies she liked. Kelly had a sudden epiphany as to Jay's intentions. Jay's gift to her was not necessarily a pink box full of kept promises; Jay's gift to her was the experience she was now having and the way it was making her feel.

Kelly could not wait to get home and go to her bedroom to explore the pink box and discover what other treasure it contained. She took out the kept promises one by one, throwing the yellow ball at Mildred, who seemed to smile knowingly, except Kelly knew that dogs do not smile. She read the Valentine's Day card, in which Jay had written a nice, sweet note. Eventually, all the way down at the bottom of the pink box, hidden under the box that contained the magic tablet, she found the envelope. Kelly recognized the handwriting immediately, just as she had recognized his cologne upon opening the lid. She also recognized the instrument with which her name had been written on the outside of the envelope. It was the rather large, classic fountain pen that Jay kept on his desk. The black pen with the rich black ink that Jay had used to write each and every note he had ever written her. She then realized that this was the real reason why Jay had sent her the pink gift box via carrier pigeons. The contents of the envelope, good or bad, was the reason she had been sent on such a wonderful adventure.

With slightly trembling hands, Kelly opened the envelope and saw within it three pieces of paper. One was a note of gratitude, one was a note of proof, and one offered a proposition for cognitive consideration that within it contained yet one more kept promise. All the writing on the papers was done with the same pen, in the same rich black ink, and with words and phrases that were put together in a rather peculiar way but easily conveyed the message. She read the thank-you note first in which Jay expressed his gratitude for her visit and for the way that she had made him feel. The note of proof showed the order date of the magic tablet. Kelly noted that it had been ordered before she met Jay. The magic tablet had been ordered the night she was traveling from the land of the cowboys back to God's country, when she told Jay that she had not yet read the chapters he had sent her, as the font appeared way too small on her phone. Upon hearing Kelly's statement, Jay had mentioned to her that such inconveniences would not do, and that he would remedy the situation. At the time, Kelly did not quite understand what Jay meant, but now she did.

The third note offered a conundrum in the form of a proposition. Jay reminded Kelly of something he had done even before he met her. Kelly had once told Jay how despondent she had been the previous year when her lover at the time did not prioritize her on a most important event for her: Valentine's Day dinner. Upon hearing her say that, Jay had made certain arrangements so that he could whisk her away to the last island at the end of the overseas highway, to his preferred hotel there. He had also made reservations at his favorite restaurant for the two of them to have Valentine's Day dinner together, together. Jay had mentioned these plans to her during one of their dinners at a wonderful local bistro, on one of the first four heavenly days during her visit.

Kelly had since forgotten Jay telling her about this plan. However, upon reading the third note, the memory of that lovely dinner with Jay came rushing back. Kelly vividly remembered where they sat—at a table for two outside on the sidewalk—and how she had petted a passerby's dog because of how much that dog reminded her of Mildred. Kelly remembered how close to Jay she felt that night. That while walking back from the restaurant, she had reached for Jay's hand. Kelly remembered how they walked back mostly in silence, hand in hand. This was the first time they had held hands while walking together.

On that third piece of paper, Jay reminded Kelly of the plans he had made for the two of them for Valentine's Day dinner. All she had to do was say she wished it and he would make it happen. She could either come to him the Friday night before and they would drive down together on Saturday morning, or, as an acceptable alternative, he would arrange it so that she could be brought down to him at the island by air, land, or sea. Her choice. Jay also mentioned in his note that he would be going down there anyway, either to be with her or to ponder on what could have been. He ended by saying that whatever she decided, he wanted her to know that Jay and Kelly were, had always been, and would always be good.

Upon reading the words that Jay had written in the third note, Kelly was immediately conflicted. The idea sounded divine, and the plan excited her, but she paused. She paused for the same reason that she had always paused when it came to him. Although she did not remember, she had paused for this same reason thousands of times before when it came to Jay, in thousands of past lives and parallel universes. The issue was always the same: Jay had been sent to her in the wrong gift box, and further partaking of that forbidden fruit would bring up the same temptations and the same emotional angst that a mere few months earlier she had run away from. Now that she was emotionally stabilizing, Kelly wondered if she would dare get close to that fire again.

The next day, Kelly felt compelled to text Jay and tell him nice things about what she hoped for his day and reiterate how good her adventure had made her feel. She even ventured to confess that she liked him a lot. His answers were immediate, as always, and used the same peculiar phraseology and association of words that were customary for him. Kelly almost felt as if she was communicating with a reflection of herself in a mirror, which immediately allayed any fears that she thought of and would bring up. It then occurred to Kelly that texting with Jay was almost like texting with a magic soul mirror. She chuckled at this thought because she was reminded of one day when Jay pointed at a mirror that he had placed behind his bedroom door and told her it was a magic mirror. When Kelly looked at herself in it, she looked considerably taller and slimmer. When Jay asked her if she knew how the mirror had been made magic, she told him she did, as carnivals had been a passion for her as a child. Kelly proceeded to explain how it was done. Upon hearing her answer, Jay smiled and told her that he was most impressed.

When Kelly asked Jay why he had placed the magic mirror behind his bedroom door, he told her it was because he wanted a daily reminder of a lesson he had learned years prior. Jay explained that he had come to learn that sometimes perception was just as important as reality, at times even more so. That although our objective evaluation of ourselves is important, the way we think about ourselves is at times even more so. Jay further elucidated that he wanted a daily reminder that if at any time we desire to change or improve ourselves in any way, it is extremely important for us to be able to visualize our end goal, and then manifest it as a reality in all our thoughts, words, and deeds. Kelly understood Jay's perspective, as by now she knew that Jay viewed reality as having dual manifestations. One was objective and concrete, and the other was less defined, more of a matter of interpretation, and existed in a realm where all spoken phrases were poetry, romance was the connective fabric, and an inspiring soundtrack always played in the background. Kelly knew that Jay preferred to exist in that second realm. This peculiar way in which Jay saw the world around him and his ability to uniquely express it were qualities that Kelly found fascinating about him. It was one of the reasons Kelly always felt a certain irresistible, enigmatic, deep attraction toward Jay, despite her Herculean efforts to suppress it.

Kelly went on her wonderful pink box adventure on Tuesday. By Wednesday evening, she still had not made up her mind as to what she wanted to do about Jay's provocative proposition. Seeking help and advice on the matter, Kelly brought up the subject to her sister Kylie and her friend Cheryl. She spoke to them about the adventure, the pink box, the offer, and her misgivings about it. To her sister, she had to clarify a certain white lie about Jay and how she had come to know him. She divulged to her who he was and explained how he had come to her in the wrong gift box. Kelly asked Kylie to promise that she would not tell their parents. After all, they would never understand.

In this life, Kelly had been born of a very nurturing and caring disposition, and after she thought about the above considerations, she immediately thought about Jay, as his thoughtfulness and attentiveness were very endearing. Kelly felt that she and Jay would be lifelong friends, as he had told her as much. The last thing she wanted to do was hurt him. Kelly had tried to explain this to Jay on the fifth night of her visit, when she informed him that she had decided to leave, as further interactions with Jay were likely to result in heartache for them both. He had shown strength that night. Jay acknowledged that she could indeed hurt him but that it would be okay, as he would get by. From the words he said to her, Kelly somehow felt as if Jay was speaking in the past tense from prior personal experience, almost as if she had already hurt Jay before, perhaps thousands of times before. However, at the same time, Kelly got the inkling that if she were to ever hurt Jay, no matter how many times and how deep the pain, that he would gladly take the risk at the chance to be with her again. Kelly had this strange feeling, as if she had lived through this situation with Jay before—many times before. Undeterred and full of optimism, he kept coming back to her again and again.

Kelly also thought that by now Jay had built some credibility with her. He had been strong on that fifth night when she told him that she wanted to leave. On the sixth day and night of her visit, he did not make a scene or get angry or resentful, but rather was nice and loving and helped pack her things so that she could go. As he had promised, he did not lift a finger to try to stop her. Thinking about it now, Kelly almost wished that Jay had not made letting her go seem so easy. She wished that he would have fought a little harder to try to convince her to stay. Moreover, when Kelly decided to leave and asked Jay to give her some space for her to sort out her thoughts, he had complied as per her wishes and had not pestered her or reached out unless she did so first. After this last proposal, he had not mentioned it again, nor had he tried to convince her or influence her decision in any way. Besides, she knew he was going to go on the trip either way, with or without her. All these thoughts swirled in Kelly's head and made it hard for her to come to a final decision as to what to do about Jay's offer. Still conflicted, Kelly went to bed on Wednesday after deciding to sleep on it overnight. She hoped that in the morning, she would begin to see the light as to what she should do regarding Jay's offer.

By Thursday morning after considerable consideration and various vacillations, Kelly finally made up her mind. She decided to decline the adventure, no matter how much she wanted to partake. She planned to call Jay that morning and kindly refuse his kind offer, no matter how tempting. And so, she did. Kelly called Jay first thing, when she knew he would be shaving prior to his morning shower, as by now she knew that Jay was a creature of habit and could tell with almost absolute certainty where he would be at just about any time of the day. Jay answered with the same attitude he always displayed toward her. It was a mixture of tenderness and kindness that becomes comforting and familiar between lovers after a while. When Kelly struggled to say what she intended to say and refuse his offer, Jay prompted Kelly to speak her mind without fear. He reminded her that Jay and Kelly were, had always been, and would always be good. Jay told Kelly that whatever she decided, he would readily accept it without any protestations.

Talking to Jay that morning, somehow Kelly found herself unable to tell him that she wanted to decline his invite. She felt one last twinge of hesitation before making her final decision. Kelly had intended to tell Jay that she was going to kindly refuse his kind offer. However, to the contrary, Kelly inexplicably heard herself utter words that were the total opposite of her intentions. Kelly heard herself say that she would indeed go with him to the last island on the overseas highway, to his favorite hotel there, and on Valentine's Day she was going to let Jay take her to his favorite restaurant on the island for a special Valentine's Day dinner. By then Kelly was committed; by then she was trapped.

To her own surprise Kelly found herself packing again for yet another trip, but for a shorter stay this time. She flew in on Friday night into the tropical city by the sea, as they were to set off on their adventure on Saturday morning. Seeing Jay again was like seeing a long-lost friend. She recognized his scent, his touch, his aura. He felt comfortable, like home, like the special pillow and blanket that Kelly always traveled with and used to sleep every night.

On Saturday morning the two of them left in Jay's topless carriage and headed south, beyond the confines of the land that protrudes into the sea and onto the string of small islands that lay beyond. They took the overseas highway on their way to the last island along that chain. The trip was heavenly. The weather was perfect as they enjoyed the warmth of the morning sun and the brisk wind in their faces as they drove. The music that Jay played reminded Kelly of the music that was popular in God's country, which somehow felt uniquely appropriate for their trip. It almost seemed like this was something they had done before. It almost seemed as if this was the way it had always been.

When Kelly asked Jay if he had planned activities for them during their trip, he told her that indeed he had, but that he also wanted her input in the decision-making. To that end, Jay told Kelly that during the trip, he would point to a series of options of things they could do so that she could decide. These would be like forks in the road, and she would be given two options to choose from. Jay told her it was his responsibility to present the options; it was hers to decide among the options presented.

Kelly could tell that Jay was relaxed and happy the entire trip down. He explained to her about the geography of the area and was quick to point out interesting landmarks he wanted Kelly to see and experience. Somewhere about halfway between here and there, Jay announced that it was time for lunch and presented Kelly with the first fork in the road in the form of two potential restaurants from which she was supposed to choose. One option was a large buffet-style eatery with windows that looked out onto a small beach. The other was a quainter, open-air restaurant named after a fish found in the waters of that region. That establishment had dining tables on a second-floor veranda and was adjacent to a marina where a multitude of colorful fishing vessels were docked. Kelly originally chose the larger restaurant, but the wait was too long, so they moved on to the other option. As they sat on a high table on the veranda eating in the nice, cool breeze, Jay confessed that he would have preferred for Kelly to have chosen this restaurant initially, as he had always envisioned the two of them eating there. He further explained that it is not unusual for one to make the wrong decision when presented with a fork in the road. However, he shared with Kelly his strong belief that thankfully, sometimes God intervenes and points in the direction one needs to go.

A little while after continuing their drive, Jay and Kelly crossed a long bridge that went on for miles and offered a wonderful panoramic vista of a royal-blue sky framing a clear turquoise sea on which multiple motor and sail boats lazily traveled to their respective destinations. The view from high atop a section of the bridge seemed like a tropical paradise, the kind of scene conducive to transcendent thoughts and sublime dreams. Kelly, feeling the sun on her face and the wind in her hair, got caught up in the emotional wave of the moment and exquisitely enjoyed the last half of their trip to their destination.

Those who travel the overseas highway orient themselves by whatever mile marker they are on. All along the trip, Jay had pointed out to Kelly the mile markers that were of significance to him. He showed her where his friends lived, where he usually went fishing, where he would like to take her in the future to glide across the water. Suddenly, around mile marker twenty-nine, Jay pulled off to the side of the road, stopped his carriage adjacent to a small bridge, and pointed east toward the horizon. Jay told Kelly that if he were to put an enchanted island anywhere in the world, he would choose that spot. It would be a little island full of palm trees that was like an oasis in the desert, but exclusively for lovers. Talking in riddles again, Jay suggested that if Kelly closed her eyes tight and allowed her heart to believe, such a place would one day exist for them, and he would take her there for a future Valentine's Day dinner. Caught up in the moment, Kelly closed her eyes and wished it so. Upon opening her eyes and looking into Jay's, she got the feeling that he somehow had willed the island to already be there. She got the strange premonition that at one point in the future she would be presented with another fork in the road, and that one of the two paths she was to choose from ended up with her and Jay being there, in that little island full of palm trees, located somewhere in the middle of the ocean upon which her eyes now gazed.

While mutually marinating on thoughts about the little island, Jay and Kelly continued their drive and finally made it to their destination by early afternoon. They checked into bungalow eighteen at Jay's favorite hotel on the last island at the end of the overseas highway. Kelly immediately realized why Jay liked it there. The bungalow's veranda was located within six steps of an inviting kidney-shaped pool, which was itself located in what seemed like a miniature Garden of Eden. After she inquired, Jay explained to Kelly that he came there often, usually alone, because it was a place where he could find peace. He could quiet his mind there so as to be able to think and write. Kelly understood, as she began to feel a sense of peace overtake her too.

After settling in, they both changed and went to the pool for a while. While there, they were served plastic glasses full of wine, which tasted heavenly and felt relaxing after their trip. Eventually, Jay suggested they get dressed and go to dinner. They ventured out in the town, where Kelly chose a restaurant that offered an inviting menu of edibles from the sea. They had dinner as in their first four days together. They ate, talked, laughed, touched. As they strolled, chatting on their way back to the hotel, they heard music coming from a bar named after an unkempt man, which was about half a block away. Kelly was thanking Jay for the box full of kept promises that he had gifted her days prior, when Jay asked her if she remembered any of the promises that she had made to him—particularly those that she had not yet kept.

Kelly was taken aback by his question because as far as she knew, in this life she had never made any promises to Jay, let alone promises that she had not kept. Jay then reminded her that he had a special photographic memory when it came to her, and that he would never forget anything she had ever told him. After she looked at him inquisitively, Jay reminded her how she had mentioned in their first four days together that she was going to cook for him one day, that she would go grocery shopping for them one day, that she would buy a bathroom carpet for him one day. As Jay rattled off these items, Kelly did remember she had said those things, but she did not necessarily consider them promises per se, but rather off-the-cuff comments made in passing. When she asked him if there were any others, Jay told her that there was one more: she had promised him that she would dance with him one day.

As Jay said this, he took her hand and guided her inside the bar named after an unkempt man, from which the music was emanating. As Kelly followed Jay in what seemed the direction of the dance floor, Kelly's first thought was to question what Jay would think of her dancing. She had been a tall, athletic girl all her life, but she never considered herself a great dancer. Quickly thereafter, she worried about what she would think of *his* dancing, and of what they would look like dancing together. She hoped for the best as Jay pulled her onto the dance floor. Kelly reminded herself that this place—this last island at the end of the overseas highway—was thousands of miles away from God's country. It was far, far away from where she grew up and from anyone she knew. Being there with Jay was almost like being with him on a deserted island, where there were no people around. A place where no one would judge her.

As Kelly let go of her fears and inhibitions, she embraced the moment and began to feel the rhythm of the music. Now, feeling increasingly more comfortable, Kelly concentrated on Jay in the hope that at least he could hold his own. Ever since high school, Kelly had been utterly disappointed and at times embarrassed by the dancing skills of the men she had been involved with. She hoped Jay would not follow this disappointing streak and embarrass her or make her feel uncomfortable as they danced together. Then she realized that Jay had music in his soul. Jay was dancing not only as if no one was watching, but as if he did not care if they were, almost as if he was daring them to. Jay was feeling the music, the rhythm…living the moment. Kelly then realized yet another reason why Jay was so appealing to her. She felt that for the first time, she had gotten a glimpse at the treasure hidden deep inside the box, underneath all the other boxes containing kept promises. It was at that moment that Kelly got her first true glimpse of Jay's eternal spirit. Kelly realized that Jay danced like he lived: inspired, fearless—free.

The following morning Jay took Kelly to the best breakfast place on the island. They ate and drank the most delicious meal while surrounded by roosters heralding the start of a brand-new day. A day full of promise and possibilities. Afterward, Jay walked Kelly toward what he said was the old home of his favorite writer. As they approached the house, Jay presented Kelly with yet another fork in the road. It was her choice as to whether they go tour the house or lounge outside in the garden of a beautiful grand hotel that was not too far away. Kelly sensed that Jay for some reason wanted her to see that house; she chose that option.

Upon entering the grounds, Kelly felt a special joy at being there. She was struck by the many cats that inhabited the place. Kelly took care of her sister's cat once and did not much like the experience. She swore that she would never own one. However, these cats were friendly, beautiful, and somehow she did not find them objectionable. Perhaps because she learned that they were special cats, some of which had six toes per paw. These cats' imperfections were honestly displayed and evident for the whole world to see. This made Kelly feel a certain kinship with them. When Jay suggested that they take a guided tour of the house, Kelly agreed. While waiting for the official tour to commence, Jay, who had visited the house before, showed Kelly the grounds the house was on. He showed her the pet cemetery, the peculiar cat fountain, the author's writing studio, and the penny that was embedded in the concrete by the pool, and told her of its significance.

A few minutes later, while sitting on a bench on the veranda waiting for the tour group to gather, Jay informed Kelly that the open area to the side of the house, just in front of where they sat, was regularly used for functions and weddings. Kelly casually asked Jay if he wished that one day he would be married there. Without the slightest hesitation, almost as if he had been thinking about it the entire day, Jay answered that he always saw himself getting married somewhere in God's country. When she further inquired if he planned to marry quickly in one of the courthouses there, Jay said that no, he envisioned getting married in one of the many small, tall-steepled churches that he knew were quite common in that area. When Jay said this, Kelly felt her heart skip several beats. If she would have been standing, her knees would have buckled.

The tour of the house was most informative, as Kelly learned about the life, times, and sad demise of Jay's favorite writer. She had not recalled his name when mentioned nor any of the books he had written, but Jay assured her that she had most likely read some of his works during her junior high and high school years. As they traveled from room to room of the house, listening to interesting anecdotes about its inhabitants and previous owner, they came upon a certain room that Kelly found most interesting, and which she sensed also held a special curiosity for Jay.

In that room, the tour guide pointed to a picture on the wall of the writer when he was nineteen years of age. He was photographed in a hospital bed and seemed to have one of his legs in a cast. The tour guide explained that the writer had sustained war injuries during World War I in Italy, while driving an ambulance carrying wounded soldiers to a field hospital. He had stayed for months at a hospital, recovering, when he met and fell in love with one of his nurses, an English woman named Agnes. Eventually their romance ended when Agnes sent him a "dear writer" letter informing him that she did not love him, and that she was soon to marry another. The resulting heartache inspired the writer to create a most heartfelt novel regarding that experience. In essence, nurse Agnes became the writer's muse.

In the book, the writer had named himself Frederic and gave the nurse the name Catherine. Kelly learned the book had been published close to a century ago and became the writer's first bestseller. The book, now considered an American classic, had since been adapted numerous times to theater, television, and film. Upon hearing the story told, Kelly looked over at Jay, who seemed engrossed in the tour guide's words and did not notice her glance. For a second, Kelly felt that there had been a hidden message in the experience of that room for her. Carried away by the moment, she secretly hoped that someday, like nurse Agnes, she would inspire someone to write a story about her. Kelly hoped that someday she would become someone's muse. The tour group was then ushered into another room and Kelly, distracted, thought no more of it.

Once the tour was over, Jay and Kelly returned to the hotel where they spent some relaxing pool time followed by a sumptuous lunch and the most delicious fish dip that either of them had ever tasted. While they both sipped on refreshing, magnificent margaritas with plenty of salt along the rim, Jay mentioned to Kelly that she looked spectacularly stunning in her new white bikini, cover-up, and floppy hat. He further told her that from that moment on and forever more, he would always remember her whenever he drank tequila. Upon hearing his words, Kelly felt beautiful, empowered, invincible. Once back at the hotel, Kelly went to take a nap while Jay returned to the pool. Late afternoon, upon waking up from her nap most refreshed, Kelly decided to join Jay at the pool for a bit. After a while, she excused herself and went to take a shower and get ready for dinner.

For their Valentine's Day dinner, Jay had made reservations for the two of them at what he said was his favorite restaurant on the island. Jay had explained to Kelly that sometimes when he went fishing with his friends, he would often bring back his best catch and the chef at the restaurant would prepare it for him. They would serve it to him at the bungalow's veranda, where he would eat it by the pool in the late afternoon breeze.

When Kelly inquired as to how she should dress, Jay told her that the island was very informal but as this was a special occasion, she should be able to wear the pink dress that she never got to use the year prior, as she had been soundly disappointed when her Valentine's dinner plans had been canceled last minute. Jay further mentioned that he intended to wear his blazer, as the occasion demanded a measure of formality. Kelly was excited about dressing up for Valentine's Day dinner. She always liked playing dress-up. With her hair down, the right dress, and the right heels, she always felt powerful. When she could deal with men eye to eye, she knew she had girl oogle power over them.

When Jay got out of the shower, upon seeing her, he paused. Showing signs of liking what he saw, he told her she looked stunning and came to her and kissed her. Jay told Kelly that she looked like California; however, whenever he touched her, she felt to him more like Carolina. Once again, Kelly beamed and overflowed with confidence. She knew that she had power over him.

Jay was as simple in dress as he was complex of mind. He was dressed quickly, and soon they walked through the threshold of their bungalow on their way to his favorite restaurant, where Jay had made a reservation for the two of them to have Valentine's Day dinner together, together.

When Kelly inquired whether they would be driving to the restaurant, Jay told her that it would not be necessary, as the restaurant was close by. They walked out one of the side doors of the hotel and once on the sidewalk, Jay guided Kelly to the right. After a mere half-block to the right again, he pulled a door and announced that they were there. Kelly was confused at first and thought that Jay was taking her back to the hotel lobby. However, she then realized that although the restaurant had the same name as the hotel they were staying at, it was not connected to the hotel lobby in any way. Kelly thought the restaurant was quaint and lovely. She immediately saw why Jay liked it. It fit his character—simple, tasteful, elegant. The staff seemed to know him there and they were soon ushered to a table for two by the window.

Jay and Kelly had a wonderful Valentine's Day dinner. They ordered a bottle of Bordeaux, which tasted like the nectar of the sweetest fruits found on Earth. They had the most wonderful gluten-free meal, which consisted of prime rib, duck, and mixed vegetables. They ate, talked, laughed, touched. They loved.

In this life, Kelly had been born chatty. This night, however, she did not want to speak. She just wanted to listen and learn as much about Jay as she could. She sat there fascinated, mesmerized, as she listened. Kelly found herself falling deeper and deeper into a bottomless abyss. Jay in turn, animated and full of energy, talked. There were secrets he wanted to share, there were things he wanted her to know now that he had found her.

In this life, Jay had been born an introvert. He was allotted a meager number of words that he felt compelled to utter each day. Today, however, he had been very relaxed spending time with Kelly. Today, Jay had not uttered too many words and it seemed he had saved the rest of his daily allotment for their dinner. Jay had a lot of things he wanted and needed Kelly to know, and he told her. He spoke of secrets, the ones he kept in his heart. Jay was animated that night in the way he talked, gestured, and the way he looked at her. He displayed a boundless energy that would not be denied.

Upon returning to bungalow eighteen after their meal, Kelly and Jay went to the pool for a while, talked some more, held hands, kissed, and eventually made their way back inside. Overcome by the evening, Kelly looked at Jay in a most peculiar way while he talked. When Jay realized this, he paused as if he sensed that Kelly had something to say. Kelly asked Jay to please excuse her, that sometimes words failed her. Jay gently smiled, grabbed her face in his hands, and kissed her lips, her face, her scars. He told her that it was not her job to come up with the words; that was his role. It was her role to listen to them, to feel them, and if so moved, to live them.

Kelly then looked up at Jay and uttered the first words that came to her heart. Kelly asked Jay to please make love to her. Without saying another word and without hesitation, as if he was commanded by God himself, Jay obediently and lovingly complied. He held her in his arms, said those things that only he could say, and made love to her with reckless abandon and such passion as Kelly had never experienced. Jay made love to Kelly as if he had just found the true love of his eternal life and had gotten her to see who he was. Jay made love to Kelly with every fiber of his being until there was nothing left, having spent all of himself on her.

Kelly allowed herself to let go of all inhibitions and exquisitely enjoy the magic of the moment. It did not take long for her to experience a certain state of enhanced consciousness that she knew existed, but which had a summit she had not yet reached before. When he took her there, Kelly was most grateful to Jay and expressed her gratitude instinctively, viscerally, by kissing every part of him that her lips could reach, almost as if wanting to eat him and make him a part of her.

Exhausted from the effort, Jay soon fell into a deep sleep. Kelly did not sleep that night. While still experiencing the warm glow of supreme existence, Kelly was deep in thought. As she snuggled next to Jay and felt the warmth of his embrace, she could feel the rhythm of his breathing and his heart as he slept. It occurred to Kelly that she had never seen Jay sleep before. It seemed that all times she had been awake around Jay, he had been awake too. Kelly recalled that Jay was always awake when she went to sleep, and he was always awake when she woke up. It was almost as if Jay was her personal, tireless, guardian angel sent on a mission to always watch over her. Kelly was then reminded of one day when she had asked Jay from where he got his energy, his stamina. Jay answered that it all came from his joy at being alive.

Not long before their trip along the overseas highway to the last island on that road, and perhaps in preparation for it, Jay asked Kelly if she liked road trips. She remembered telling him that it depended on the duration of the trip and who she was taking the trip with. Jay then suggested that Kelly join him on the drive down but that for her return trip, he would have Kelly sent back to the balmy city by air directly, so that she would be fresh and ready for work the next day. Now Kelly felt the urge to wake Jay up and tell him that she had reconsidered the answer to his prior question. She wanted to tell him that she indeed loved road trips. Kelly wanted to wake Jay up and tell him that she wished she would be taking the drive with him back up to the tropical city by the sea and that she hoped the trip would take them a lifetime.

Lying next to Jay as he slept, feeling the warmth of his body next to hers, and with a sense of hope at the possibilities of what might be, Kelly thought about the next day due to rise with the sun in the next few hours. She felt the wings of her heart spread wide open and stretch, just like she would spread her arms wide and stretch upon awakening in the morning, ready to take on the new day. Today was sure to be a poignant day, as Kelly was extremely excited about spending it with Jay, but she was also very aware that by that evening, her Valentine's Day weekend would end, heralding some impending deep sadness. She very much knew that in the next few days that would follow, when she found herself alone without Jay by her side, that sadness would undoubtedly creep in, creating turbulence in her mind and heart, making her feel as if she was not herself.

Jay and Kelly spent a relaxing, heavenly time in the pool again that morning and then went out for a late lunch at a restaurant named after a sound. After a wonderful lunch and refreshing, magnificent margaritas with plenty of salt on the rim, Kelly expressed to Jay how this had been a most magical weekend, and she thanked him for allowing her to experience it. She asked him if there was any wish that she could grant him, anything that she could do for him to make the weekend as magical for him as it had been for her. Jay assured Kelly that she had already granted him such a wish, as making her happy was the one thing sure to make him happy.

Upon hearing his words, Kelly told Jay that in all her life, she was not aware that guys like him existed, that guys like him were real. Jay responded by saying that most men, maybe even all men, were like him, except that they had to be inspired to show that side of themselves. Jay was sure that all men had that in them. What she was seeing in his behavior had been solely inspired by her. Jay explained to Kelly that although he did not intend or plan for this to happen when he first answered her siren call, she had touched him deep in his heart and had brought out this side of him, without him wishing or willing it to be so. Jay was living inspired, and it was because of her.

Kelly yearned to know and asked Jay to please explain what living inspired meant in a way that she could understand. Jay paused in deep thought for a while, as if to find the right words. He explained that living inspired meant existing in a magical state of being, an enhanced level of consciousness in which the realm of possibilities was limitless. Living inspired, one could not only surmise what was and what is, but also the multiple possibilities to make the current "is" into the future one would want it to be. Living inspired meant that one can see sounds, hear taste, smell touch...live dreams. He expressed his wish for her to someday experience that feeling. Preferably inspired by him, but if not by him, then by someone else, as she was truly deserving of it. Jay assured Kelly once again that just like her, he had experienced a magical weekend as well.

On the way back to their hotel, Jay and Kelly walked leisurely but silently for a while, as if each of them in their own minds was pondering possibilities. Their bodies involuntarily migrated closer and closer to one another as they walked, pulled by the greatest gravitational force known to creation. Soon, their shoulders were almost touching when simultaneously, their hands reached out for one another—each finding a willing hand waiting, eager to be held. As Jay and Kelly walked back toward the hotel, they walked side by side and hand in hand as friends, lovers...partners. They walked as one.

The rest of the afternoon was as enjoyable as the first four heavenly days they had initially spent together in the tropical city by the sea, except compressed into a couple of sublime hours. As the time of departure got closer, they started getting their things together for their trip back. Jay was to take his topless carriage back to the tropical city by the sea. Kelly would be whisked away by air to the balmy city by the gulf. Kelly mentioned to Jay how bad she felt that he was taking the road trip back alone, and that she was going back by air only because he had insisted on it. Jay responded by saying she need not worry. That whether in a magic carpet or in the seat next to him on his carriage on his way back, she would be with him either way. Jay explained that was because there would not be a single second of that road trip back when he would not be thinking about her.

As Jay made the last turn into the airport to drop her off, Kelly thanked Jay for changing her mind about coming on this trip. Jay seemed surprised and reminded her that she had never refused his invitation. If she would have, he assured her that he would have accepted her answer and would not have tried to convince her to change her mind in any way, as he valued her judgment and respected her decisions when she made him aware of them. Jay shared with Kelly that when she abruptly left the tropical city by the sea months before, he had felt unsettled because he did not feel that Kelly had gotten to know him as he was. Their initial time spent together had been a bit awkward, as they had just met and there were logistical issues that clouded their true selves from one another. However, after spending this weekend with her, and after taking her to Valentine's Day dinner, Jay felt that he was able to fully display himself to Kelly as he truly was.

Jay explained that he was satisfied he had done everything in his power to allow Kelly to see him as he was, as he could be when living inspired, and how he loved. He told her that he was satisfied that, both by words and deeds, he had conveyed to her how he felt toward her in the deepest recesses of his heart. He further explained that since it had been she who had gotten scared and ran away, their love could only be realized if she decided of her own accord to return to him. She fully knew his preference for how he wanted things to go between them going forward. However, he wanted her to make her decision as to what to do about him, about them, undisturbed and without any meddling from him.

Jay promised Kelly that he would not reach out or chase after her in any way. Moreover, he said she need not worry that he would ever show up to her morning walk unannounced. He would abide by her decision, no matter what she chose, as he always saw her as his equal, his lover—his partner. Jay let Kelly know in no uncertain terms that whatever happened next between the two of them, it was now solely up to her. Finally, he reminded her that they were, had always been, and would always be good.

Less than an hour later, Kelly found herself in her seat on the magic carpet as it moved slowly to get in line for takeoff. In her hands, she held a pink box. Kelly thought back to three days before, when they had arrived at Jay's favorite hotel in the last island at the end of the overseas highway. After being given the keys to bungalow eighteen, Jay walked Kelly to it and showed her where it was. As per usual, Kelly was expecting Jay to open the door to the bungalow to usher her in, but this time he merely pointed it to her, gave her the keys, and directed her to please make herself at home there, while he went to the carriage to get their things.

Kelly found Jay's behavior slightly odd, but she thought that perhaps he was worried about their luggage being left out in the street on their topless carriage, where they might inadvertently disappear. Thus, Kelly did as instructed. She let herself into a beautifully decorated, cozy, one-room cottage with an immaculate bathroom. As she reached for her phone to take a picture of the room, she noticed the red roses sitting on what would for the next couple of days be her nightstand. She initially thought the flowers were part of the room decoration, particularly since this was Valentine's Day weekend. However, when she bent down to smell the roses, Kelly saw clipped to one of the stems a card with her name on it. Upon reading it, she realized that the roses had been sent by Jay.

When Jay got back to the bungalow with their things, Kelly felt the urge to kiss him and thank him. As she did, she became acutely aware that arrangements had been arranged and rearranged so as to optimize this experience for her. Kelly came to know that this Valentine's Day weekend, she was being highly prioritized. She was deeply moved and very much appreciated Jay's efforts and told him so.

Jay and Kelly proceeded to unpack their things. As she organized her belongings in the bungalow, Kelly had the occasion to walk in and out of the bathroom several times. She did not notice it at first, but soon became aware of a pink box that had materialized right next to the flowers.

Kelly had already experienced a wonderful adventure related to a pink box from Jay days before. She felt excitement well up in her as she grabbed it and called Jay's attention to it. With a big smile on her face, Kelly extended her arms as if to show him the treasure she was holding. Upon seeing Kelly do this, Jay knowingly smiled at the confirmation that carrier pigeons had once again found their intended target. Jay explained that the pink box contained her Valentine's Day gifts, but that there was one catch: she could not open the pink box until she was on the magic carpet on her way back to the balmy city by the gulf. Jay further explained that the pink box contained three separate gifts. Two were in the form of envelopes and the third one was not, but that she could not open this third gift until she was sure that her magic carpet's wheels were off the ground and she was already in the air.

Throughout the following three days, Kelly's mind kept coming back to the pink box, wondering all the while what its contents could be. She experienced a multitude of emotions that weekend, but the intrigue about the box was omnipresent. Now, sitting on the runway getting ready to take off, Kelly ventured to open the pink gift box. After all, Jay had told her she could open it and look at the presents as soon as she was on the magic carpet. The only rule that Jay had mentioned beyond that was that she could not explore the third present, the one that was not in an envelope, until the magic carpet wheels had left the ground. In this life, Kelly had been born a person who follows rules, and she was intent on following the instructions she had been given.

Just like her first experience with the previous pink box, as soon as she opened it, she smelled Jay's cologne, the memory of him becoming more vivid because of it. In the box, there were three separate items: two were envelopes with her name written on them in the same rich black ink that he used for every note he had ever written her. The third item was several pieces of paper stapled together and folded. Kelly looked at the envelopes and carefully opened each one in turn. The first envelope contained the answer to a question. The second envelope contained information as to a particular place and time where Jay would not be present.

Kelly remembered that in one of the many conversations she had with Jay during those first four heavenly days they spent together in the tropical city by the sea, upon hearing Jay explain some of the magical tricks he had learned over a considerable amount of schooling and apprenticeship, Kelly had asked Jay facetiously if he had learned how to turn back time. Jay casually responded that indeed he had. When she asked him to explain further, Jay mentioned that the information was a highly guarded trade secret—that he would divulge it to her eventually, but only when he got to know her better and was sure that she could be trusted. In the first envelope, Jay explained this highly guarded trade secret and attached a lifetime gift certificate that would allow Kelly to partake of it any time she wanted to in the future.

The second envelope was a bit confusing to Kelly at first because if anything, she had thought it would contain another invitation or a proposition as to when and where she and Jay could see each other again. Kelly fully expected Jay to include a cryptic message or invitation to their next adventure together. However, this envelope was most perplexing, as it showed a time and a place where Jay informed Kelly that he would not be present. The time was about two months into the future, and the place was a familiar one she had once visited and spent four heavenly days before the two sad ones. Having Jay direct her to his abode at a time that he would not be there did not make sense at first, until Kelly read a line on the note that mentioned something about choosing one of the Jessicas.

Kelly then remembered another conversation she had had with Jay during those heavenly first four days. Kelly had mentioned to Jay that while in the tropical city by the sea, she wanted to invite her friend Jessica from the city by the great lake, as she had never visited the tropical city by the sea but was eager to do so. The second Jessica obviously referred to one of Kelly's two sisters, with whom she had—one day prior—partaken of an extremely heart-warming bonding experience—in great part due to the most amazing coincidence, and in some part due to Jay's doing. In essence, Jay was offering Kelly the opportunity to take either her friend Jessica or her sister to the tropical city by the sea and stay at his castle in the clouds, during a time that he would not be there.

As the meaning of the second gift became obvious, Kelly marveled at how Jay had a way of doing these things that were not clear at face value but somehow became apparent days, weeks, indeed years later. She mused that Jay was somewhat witty and was reminded how that appealed to her. She had always thought that smart was sexy. However, as she thought about this, she pondered on an enigma. Surely Jay had cleverly included in her Valentine's Day gifts some form of hidden message or invite as to where they would see each other again, just as he had done when he presented his invitation to this trip. Goodness, he had told her how he felt for her and how much he wished he could see her again. After further searching and some consideration, Kelly came to the realization that he had not included such a message in the pink box.

Kelly then thought back to a mere one hour ago when Jay had dropped her off. After thanking her for giving him the opportunity to take her on this Valentine's Day adventure, Jay had specifically told Kelly that although he desperately wished to see her again, he would not do anything to try to influence her decision as to whether she wished it so as well. He explicitly told her that whatever happened next between the two of them, the decision was now solely hers. Jay promised Kelly that he would not make any further overtures or reach out to her in the future unless she first requested him to do so. Kelly believed without question that Jay was telling her the truth, as she very well knew how important it was for Jay to stay true to his word and keep his promises.

It was then that Kelly came to a deeply profound epiphany. Her departure from Jay at the terminal the hour prior was the last fork in the road that Jay would present to her on that eventful trip. If she took one path, Jay would be there waiting, along with a world full of possibilities. Perhaps an enchanted little island dotted with palm trees where Jay and Kelly would have a future Valentine's Day dinner. The other path led to the end of their story…a road with a dead end, leading only to the great tragedy of potential true love left unrealized.

Perhaps Jay had indeed sent a cryptic invite after all, except it was not included in the pink box, but rather had been conveyed to Kelly days prior on their drive down, when Jay stopped at mile marker twenty-nine and told Kelly about the enchanted little island full of palm trees. As the profound implications of the decision she was facing dawned on her, Kelly gasped as if in need of air. Simultaneously, she felt the wheels of the magic carpet come off the ground.

Kelly's first instinct was to wait several seconds so that the magic carpet could gain some altitude. She then looked out the window, hoping to see Jay's topless carriage as it headed north along the overseas highway on its way to the tropical city by the sea. She did not. Kelly knew that as a physical reality, she was now in the air on a magic carpet on her way to the balmy city by the gulf. However, she also knew that in Jay's heart, she was riding with him, taking the road trip back home. Jay had told Kelly that not one second of that trip would pass that he would not be thinking about her. At this remembrance, Kelly felt her heart skip several beats. If she would have been standing, her knees would have buckled.

Bringing her attention back to the pink box that now lay on her lap, Kelly took out the third gift. She unfolded the pages, took a deep breath, and began to read the story that Jay had gifted her for Valentine's Day. As she did so, Kelly began to read *her* story.

CHAPTER 3

Frank and Betty

(Conclusion)

Frank walked through the door of the restaurant and found himself inside. He suddenly felt disoriented, momentarily losing track of where he was and the purpose of his presence there—the reason being that in the fraction of the second it took him to walk through the threshold, he had received his gift. He had been given a vision of what was happening at that same time in a parallel universe. However, his gift came with a twist; it was delivered in the wrong gift box, as it were. Upon the completion of his vision, he would not have any recollection of it. The only way that Frank would ever be cognizant of the vision he had just experienced was through another of God's great gifts: the power of imagination. God indeed played tricks sometimes. By now, Frank was used to them. He was not aware that he had just become the victim of yet another one. If he would have known, Frank would have been most grateful all the same, as he had been gifted a wonderful vision of what could have been.

In this life and at that moment, Frank was standing just past the threshold of the door of the restaurant named after another city, in a town named after someone, located halfway between here and there. Once he caught his bearings, his eyes immediately searched for Betty in the hope that he would miraculously find her sitting there waiting for him. She was not. The restaurant was almost empty. Family restaurants were not usually full the evening of Valentine's Day, as more suitable, romantic venues were the preference for this occasion. But for Frank it was different; he had planned to have his Valentine's Day dinner there, either with Betty or without her.

His eyes immediately followed the row of tables to the right of the door. The last table was empty as he hoped it would be. He directed his steps toward it while holding the pink box containing Betty's gift in his hands. Beyond where he sat was the small area where many a time Betty had taken her meals with her family. He had never been in this restaurant before but could easily recognize its interior by the picture she had sent him. That area of the restaurant had several larger tables close together and panoramic windows that looked out onto the open-air parking lot, and that at night reflected the whitish decorative bricks behind the reception area across from the front door. Above the windows, there were television sets close to the ceiling, and underneath them were cartoon paintings of mustached chefs preparing and offering their delicious concoctions. It was these peculiar paintings and the interior decorations that allowed Frank to identify this particular restaurant from one of the pictures Betty had sent him of her family after one of their dinners.

Frank chose the side of the table facing the entrance, as it would allow him to watch the door on the outside chance that Betty might walk in. She did not. He ordered food from the menu, though he did not touch it. He ordered a beer but took hardly a sip to wet his lips. Frank just sat there, holding the gift he had brought in the pink box. He looked at it in his hands and pondered. After sitting there for several minutes, hardly moving, and concentrating his thoughts on the pink box in his hands, Frank was able to slowly quiet his mind and immerse himself in deep, introspective contemplation. As he ran over and over in his head the events that had brought him there and thought of the person who had inspired him to concoct this plan no matter the poor odds of it coming to fruition, Frank's thoughts turned to the meaning of love, loving, and of being in love.

Frank concluded that love is the ultimate mechanism by which humans self-actualize, not in form but spiritually. How humans come to know that they do really exist, that they are alive in a spiritual sense. Loving is the process by which this realization takes place. It is an act that can be partaken of at will, but most times it is something that just happens to us—at times when least expected, oftentimes in the least convenient places and times. Even worse, sometimes with the least convenient people, some of whom come to us wrapped in the wrong gift boxes. The experience of being in love is plural in the sense that it requires two people. One serves to elicit the emotion while the other person experiences it. Ideally, this is a process that involves these two people simultaneously and the feelings are elicited and felt for one another. When this happens, the resulting mutual connection is nothing short of profoundly spectacular and leads to supreme, inspired living. Experiencing that feeling tastes like the nectar of the sweetest fruits found in heaven. It is a precious treasure, highly sought but seldom found.

Indeed, Frank concluded that love is to the spirit like the reflection of form in a mirror is to the mind. That reflection lets us know that we exist in form in the material world because we can see ourselves. We can see in the reflection how we look in the physical world and thereby become aware of our existence in that realm. Love is a different form of self-actualization. It is the self-actualization of our eternal spirit, as we perceive the reflection of our soul in the heart of another.

Frank sat holding a box that contained a gift for Betty which he originally thought was a story about himself. He could not write in Betty's voice because he was not fully privy to what was in Betty's heart but could only surmise it by her words and deeds. As he sat holding that pink box with the gift in it, Frank came to the epiphany that the story he had written over the past two days was not his story; it was Betty's story. Not in the sense that it was about her or that he was gifting it to her. Bur rather because upon reading it, she would be able to see the reflection of her soul in the mirror of his heart.

This realization was followed by an even more profound one. Sitting there, holding the pink box in his hands, Frank became aware that he was in love. The feeling had been inspired by Betty, but the feeling of being in love that Frank held in his heart was not hers; it was solely his. The same way that the story he held in the box in his hands was not his but hers. Frank felt an immense sense of gratitude toward Betty for bringing this feeling out in him. He knew that she did not yet recognize him for who he was, but he also knew that he would forever continue his efforts to get her to do so. Either until she recognized him or asked him to desist. Then he would do as she requested out of respect for her wishes, as he always saw her as his equal, his lover—his partner. If asked by Betty to stop, he would gracefully bow out and go away. By this point in his life, Frank had learned that true love is neither selfish nor possessive; it can only be realized if the beloved gives herself freely and willingly.

Close to two hours after he had sat down at the table, Frank felt as though he had finally reconciled his thoughts and decided it was time to leave. He yet had one more thing to do. He called the waitress over and asked her if she would be willing to grant him a most special favor. The money he offered her to comply with his request was not necessary, as the light that shone inside Frank that night was so intense, he would not be denied. He handed the pink box to the waitress and paid his bill, including the promised gigantic gratuity. Frank then walked out and back across the parking lot of the restaurant named after another city, in the town named after someone, located halfway between here and there.

As he walked in the cold snow, Frank envisioned future events. The following morning, he would leave and take a magic carpet ride back to the tropical city by the sea in which he lived. Simultaneously, the waitress who had served Frank would text Betty a picture of a pink box that she would tell her was her Valentine's Day gift, which had been left for her at the restaurant by a customer. Intrigued, excited, and living the most wonderful adventure, Betty would eventually make it to the restaurant later on that day to pick up her pink box. Upon opening it, she would find several pieces of paper stapled together and folded. She would also find an envelope with her name on it written in deep, rich black ink. Betty would recognize the envelope, ink, and handwriting, as it was the same as every note Frank had ever written her.

And so, events came to pass as Frank had envisioned. In her car, hands trembling with anticipation, Betty opened the envelope and read the note within it. Frank first expressed his gratitude to Betty for having sent her siren call and for giving him the opportunity of finding her once again. He also wrote that she needed to know that on Valentine's Day, a mere twenty-four hours prior, she had been one man's top priority above all else. In the last paragraph, Frank added that he also was including a gift. Frank reminded Betty that when they first became friends, bonded, and shared constantly—even before they met—Betty mentioned several times that she would memorialize her adventure in coming to see him, turn it into a story, and pitch it to the producers of all those romantic movies she loved to watch. In the note, Frank informed Betty that just in case meeting him had not inspired her to write such a story, he had taken the liberty of writing one for her. Frank further wrote that the gift contained within the box was her story. It was her story not because she had written it or even because he had gifted it to her, but rather because upon reading it, she would be able to behold the reflection of her soul in a mirror framed by words that came from his heart.

In this life, Betty had been born someone who is sensible and follows rules. Betty knew that it was not safe to be distracted while driving, especially on a cold day with icy roads. As she drove out of the parking lot of the restaurant named after another city, while engaged in the most wonderful adventure, Betty could not think of anything else but to get home, open the pink box, and read her story. As her car pulled out onto the street and passed in front of the hotel where Frank had slept the night before, Betty suddenly gasped as if in need of air, as she felt the jolt of the lingering energy that Frank had left behind. While doing so, Betty silently thanked God for sending someone to answer her secret prayer, even if he had been sent in the wrong gift box.

That year, Valentine's Day everywhere on Earth including God's country landed on the Lord's Day, the day before Presidents' Day. That night, as Frank put his head on his pillow, he felt overjoyed and most grateful. He felt as if God had granted him many gifts that day. His plans had not quite come to fruition as he hoped, but he had put into effect an acceptable alternative and felt good about its possibilities. Most importantly, for the first time in this life, God had allowed him the experience of having Valentine's Day dinner while being utterly in love. Moreover, God had given him the precious opportunity to thank the person who had always been meant for him for all eternity, and who had once again come into his life and brought out those exquisite emotions that lived buried deep inside him. The person who gifted Frank with the feeling of living inspired, of being in love. He thanked God for granting him the opportunity to fulfill her wish of having someone prioritize her above all on that special day, for allowing him to try to convince her to stay, and for giving him the chance to answer her secret prayer.

As Frank put his head on the pillow that night with all those thoughts swirling around his head, he felt the certainty deep in his heart that he would see Betty again, whether in this life or another. Just as this realization dawned on him, Frank felt the perception that time stood still, as to allow him to savor the existential fulfillment that he knew would never be found in any bottle or pill. Frank drifted off to sleep engulfed in a supreme state of peace, a transcendent serenity that is highly sought but seldom found.

The End

About the Author

Dr. Joe Garri started his long educational journey as a dentist who then went on to complete residency training in oral/ maxillofacial surgery. During this training program, due to his exposure to the care of patients with facial challenges such as cleft lip and palate, Dr. Garri developed a deep understanding and appreciation for how altering someone's physical appearance can have a profoundly positive impact on their psyche, self-esteem, and emotional well-being. To pursue these interests, Dr. Garri went on to complete medical school, general surgery training, and eventually a residency in plastic surgery. Besides his clinical practice where his focus is on cosmetic, craniofacial, and oral surgery, Dr. Garri remains involved in surgical education and holds academic appointments at several institutions. He very much enjoys and appreciates the time he devotes to teaching medical/dental students and surgery residents at all levels of training.

In the literary sphere, Dr. Garri's efforts include multiple scientific publications, as well as his participation as a co-editor of a textbook on craniofacial surgery, published in 2008. His exploratory journey into the realm of creative nonfiction writing culminated in Dr. Garri's first book, *Becoming a Surgeon* (self-published in 2020), which is an autobiographical account of his five years spent in general surgery residency. His second book and debut in the genre of fiction is *Valentine's Day Dinner,* a wonderful, heartwarming story about love, loving, and living inspired.

Dr. Joe Garri lives and practices plastic surgery in Miami Beach, Florida.

Websites:
Surgical practice: www.drgarri.com
Author's website: www.joegarri.com

Lightning Source UK Ltd.
Milton Keynes UK
UKHW020142020323
417877UK00002B/13/J